Mylee
in the
Mirror

Mylee
in the
Mirror

Ellie Collins

Fresh Ink Group
Guntersville

Mylee in the Mirror

Fresh Ink Group
An Imprint of:
The Fresh Ink Group, LLC
Box 931
Guntersville, AL 35976
Email: info@FreshInkGroup.com
FreshInkGroup.com

Edition 1.0   2018

Book design by Amit Dey / FIG

Cover art by Matt Collins

BISAC Subject Headings:
YAF011000   YOUNG ADULT FICTION / Coming of Age
YAF019010   YOUNG ADULT FICTION / Fantasy / Contemporary
YAF038000   YOUNG ADULT FICTION / Magical Realism

Library of Congress Control Number: 2018912386

ISBN-13: 978-1-947867-36-9 Papercover
ISBN-13: 978-1-947867-35-2 Hardcover
ISBN-13: 978-1-947867-37-6 Ebooks

Mylee
IN THE MIRROR

Chapter I

Mylee

Mylee stopped breathing. Somewhere in the back of her mind a voice screamed at her to run to safety, to flee as fast as possible. But she was frozen in place; her body refusing to listen to reason. The only thing running top speed was her racing heart.

Those eyes...those black, soulless eyes continued to bore into her as the evil mind behind them contemplated all the many ways he could cause her bodily harm. She broke into a panicked, cold sweat, despite the stuffy heat of the small space, as she imagined her painful, torturous death surely mere moments away. The highlights of her life flashed through her mind. There wasn't much there. She had just started her freshman year of high school; she was too young to die! If only she had the strength and courage to fight this terrifying foe!

He was monstrous, though, and posi-tively menacing. She wouldn't stand a chance. As she willed her voice to work, that she might at least cry out for help, the door to the attic suddenly swung open and her enemy retreated to the shadows of the eaves.

"Mylee, did you hear me?" Mom asked. "I called to you three times!"

Mylee gasped as she whipped her terrified eyes in her mother's direction. "Sorry... Sp-spider," she sputtered as she placed a hand over her chest to calm her heart and get her lungs working properly again.

Mom rolled her eyes and sighed. "Honey, I've told you a thousand times. They're much more afraid of you than you are of them. You just need to leave them alone."

Mylee was barely paying attention, though. Wishing the single hanging bulb and the dim evening light through the small window could better illuminate the area, she focused on the dark corner the vile creature of all her worst nightmares had disappeared into. She half expected him to launch back out in surprise attack. Mom didn't understand. Rational thought was not a possibility in the presence of a freaking *spider!*

"So, are we all done up here?" Mom pressed Mylee to get her mind back on task.

"Um...yeah. There's just this one more box over here," Mylee said, happily making her way in the opposite direction of the last known location of her nemesis. First assuring none of the spider's evil friends were hiding on or around the box, she picked it up and headed toward the door.

"Grammy, there was just this last box up in the attic," she announced as she made her way down the second flight of stairs, looking over the railing at her favorite person in the world, sitting in the living room.

"Let's see what we have here," Grammy Jean said anxiously, as she made a labored effort to scoot to the edge of her easy chair for a better look at this last, forgotten box.

Mylee dutifully set the box on the floor before her grandmother, sat on the floor next to it, and helped the older woman open the top.

"Oh, for Heaven's sake!" Grammy exclaimed. "I haven't seen these in years!"

"What is it?" Mylee asked as she peeked over the cardboard flap.

Grammy chuckled. "It's my hand mirror collection," she explained, as she carefully removed one of the mirrors for closer inspection. She smiled in admiration and turned the mirror around in her hands. "Oh, how Grandpa used to grumble about all the time we spent perusing garage and yard sales in search of perfect additions to my collection. He wouldn't mean a word of it, of course. Those sales are where we got his huge collection of books. He was secretly just as excited to discover a new find as I was. But you know Grandpa Doug; he never would have admitted it."

"Well he certainly found plenty of books at those sales, then! I don't think the Kirkland Library holds as many books as he had," Mylee commented, fondly remembering Grandpa sitting in his reading chair for hours on end. "Do you want to keep these?" she asked.

"No," Grammy replied with a dismissive shake of her head as she carefully returned her mirror to the box and sat back a bit in her chair. "I won't have any use for these, and my new place is just too small for anything unnecessary. You can keep any you want for yourself and the rest can go to Goodwill."

Making her way downstairs, Mom interrupted. "The attic and the upstairs bedrooms are all clear, Mom. The last of the furniture on this floor will be moved out tomorrow. Are you ready to head on out?"

Grammy Jean's relaxed smile quickly melted away. That sparkle in her eyes from discovering the long-lost box now dulled. She transformed to a picture of barely contained sorrow and regret. She took another look around the room, seeming to search desperately for any other reason to remain right where she was. Finding none, she quietly admitted, "Ready? No, but...I suppose there's nothing left to be done here. Mylee, sweetie, would you mind helping me with my walker?"

"Sure, Grammy." Mylee's somber, hushed tone matched her grandmother's.

Mylee moved the box away from the chair and grabbed Grammy's walker from the corner. Gently but firmly, she grabbed Grammy's arm and helped her up from the chair. With Mylee's steadying hand on Grammy's back, they made their way slowly and steadily toward the front door.

Mom was waiting for them at the car, holding the rear passenger-side door open, with Grammy's special cushion all set up on the seat. After assisting Grammy, Mylee ran back to grab the box and to say one more private farewell to the house that had always been just as much a home to her as the one she shared with her parents.

Everything was so still, so quiet in the house as Mylee stepped over the threshold. The front hall, once artfully decorated with a lifetime of festive snapshots and portraits, loomed stark and empty in front of her. Gone was the warmth she had associated with these walls for as long as she could remember. It was too sad to think about. Quickly grabbing the box, she headed back out, whispering a quick and quiet "goodbye" as she shut the red door with the brass knocker behind her for the last time.

After carefully placing the box in the trunk of the car, Mylee hopped in next to Grammy and Mom pulled away from the curb. She grabbed Grammy's hand and offered her a smile of support, knowing how hard this day must be for her. "I looked it up, Grammy, and there's a metro bus that runs in the afternoons from the stop at the other end of our street to the street next to the one the Kirkland Heights Retirement Home is on."

"Wonderful," Grammy responded with a smile. "I look forward to visits with you from time to time, but I don't want you to miss out on any of your activities."

"Okay, but I usually don't have much else going on after school. I have my practices on Mondays and Wednesdays, but other than that, I'm pretty free."

"Oh yes. How is your trampoline and tumbling going? Did you get moved up to the next level for next year's competitions?"

"I did for trampoline and double-mini. I'm not sure yet about tumbling, but I think so."

"I was terribly disappointed when Mylee didn't try out for high school cheerleading this fall," Mom chimed in with a shake of her head. "She would have looked amazing out there on the football sidelines. There's still time for her to try out for the winter squad, though. She could cheer the basketball team on. I just know she'd love it!"

Mylee rolled her eyes and stifled an irritated sigh. She couldn't count the number of times she and her mom had argued about cheerleading. She didn't want to get into it with her with Grammy in the car; Grammy didn't need any more stress today, of all days.

"I know cheerleading was the love of your life, Sharron, but I just don't think that's Mylee's cup of tea," Grammy said with a wink and a smile for her granddaughter.

Mylee squeezed Grammy's hand in thanks. Mom let the subject drop, probably only because they were about to pull into the retirement home parking lot. Mylee hoped her mother wouldn't remember to bring up the subject of extracurricular activities again on the way home.

* * *

It didn't take too long to get Grammy settled into her little apartment. They had already moved her furniture and belongings earlier in the day. Mylee snuggled with Grammy on her new little sofa, under the custom quilt they had gotten her as a housewarming gift. It was filled with family pictures, just in case the digital photo frame on the bedside table or the other frames Mylee had squeezed onto the sofa end tables, shelves, and cramped wall space weren't enough.

Mylee and Grammy relaxed, watching TV, laughing as they called out some right and some wrong phrases to *Wheel of Fortune* and ridiculously wrong answers to *Jeopardy*. Mom was down in the retirement home director's office, dealing with some paperwork. Mylee was thankful for the chill time with Grammy.

She hated to leave her grandmother, but after Mom finished up all she had to do and after Mylee helped Grammy with her dinner, she didn't argue when Mom said it was time to go. She had school in the morning and some homework to finish up. She hugged Grammy Jean goodbye, willing all her love and support to soak into Grammy and keep her strong until Mylee could get back, which she promised to do in a few days.

Once she and Mom were back in the car, Mylee braced herself for more badgering about trying out for the cheerleading team.

Mom surprised her with a seemingly unrelated question. "Guess who I ran into yesterday?"

"I don't know. Who?"

"Penny Smith-Martin, my high-school cheerleading squad co-captain! You know her son, Sam, right?"

"Uh...Sam Martin the football player? Yeah, I guess so. I mean...I know *of* him. It'd be pretty hard not to have heard of him at our school, but I don't *know*-him know him."

"Did you know he was recently named team captain?"

"No. I haven't really paid much attention to the football team."

"Well, you should. Much of high-school society revolves around the goings-on of the team. And from what Penny tells me, they have a real shot at the state championship again this year!"

"Good for them," Mylee said with less enthusiasm than she had hoped to offer her mother. She wondered what any of this had to do with her.

"You remember how Dad was captain of the football team in high school, too, right?"

Oh, geez, here we go, thought Mylee. "Yeaaahhhh..."

"We were on top of the world in those days. Homecoming king and queen two years in a row, voted 'Cutest Couple' senior year..." Mom's voice trailed off as she was apparently consumed by memories of high school.

Mylee didn't respond. She knew the stories all too well; she had heard them a million times. Dad was a football star. Mom was a cheerleading goddess. They were a power couple who ruled the school. She didn't know what that had to do with her. Maybe the chance meeting with her old teammate just triggered Mom to want to re-live her high-school days...again. Whatever.

She focused her attention on the view outside her window. They were about a block from home, just passing the corner with the adorable little white mission-style cottage and its bright red front door...the house they had just left hours before...Grammy's house. It looked so sad with its windows all dark, like it was mourning the loss of its owner, perhaps just as much as the owner mourned the loss of her home.

Pulling into their driveway moments later, Mylee noticed Dad wasn't home again.

She hadn't seen much of him lately. Mom seemed to have expected him to be home because upon seeing no car in the garage, she huffed and sighed. To punctuate her displeasure, she slammed her car door when she got out and stormed into the house. Not knowing what to do for Mom, Mylee carefully retrieved Grammy's box of mirrors from the trunk and made her way quietly to her room.

She'd check out the contents of the box sometime soon, but she had to get her homework finished up. Then she wanted to get to bed early. She hadn't gotten much sleep the night before. Mom and Dad's arguing had been a little louder and lasted a little longer than usual. That seemed to be the trend lately. Mylee was anxious for them to work out whatever was going on, so everything could get back to normal. Or...as normal as things could be with Grammy up at the retirement home instead of just down the street where she belonged.

Chapter II

Ty

"Get. UP!"

"Okay, okay. Sorry...I was just in the middle of a good dream and I had a hard time leaving it."

"No. I don't want to hear 'sorry', followed by one of your silly excuses. I want you *Out. Of. That. Bed!* This is the third time I've had to come in here! Third time! This is ridiculous, Ty! You have *ten* minutes before you need to be out the door and on your way to the bus stop! Don't think I'll drive you to school if you miss the bus, Mister! You can walk your butt to school if you can't get out of the house on time!"

Ty squinted a peek around his comforter after he heard the tell-tale retreating stomp of Mum's feet down the hallway, signaling it was safe. He flopped onto his back, trying to get his brain's motor running. He didn't know why Mum was so worked up; he still had a good five minutes to spare before he really had to get moving.

He didn't want to chance another tirade, though, so he sat up to prove progress, should Mum double back to give him another piece of her mind. Absently, he reached down to the floor to feel around for some clothes to throw on. If he remembered right, he had a pile nearby with his Yoda pug t-shirt on top, and it was still clean...ish. And he was pretty sure he had seen a pair of pants kicking around somewhere on his bed. Maybe they were under Pugly. He nudged his best bud, encouraging him to scoot over and...success! The pants were even warm after being slept on all night. Bonus. He was good to go.

"Mum, I'm headed out!" Ty yelled from the door a few minutes later, as he slung his backpack onto his shoulder.

"Okay. Did you feed the dog?" Mum yelled as she wiped her hands on a dish towel and made her way out of the kitchen toward the front door to give him his usual morning send-off.

"Yep."

"Put on deodorant?"

"Yep."

"I see you didn't brush your hair—again. Are you sure you don't want to just run a quick comb through it, or is that look... uh...on purpose?" Mom came closer, checking him over with a critical eye.

"It's fine, Mum."

"Uh-huh," she said with her *I-don't-approve-but-we-don't-have-time-for-it-now* scowl. "All right. Well, have a good day and I'll see you after practice," she said with a return of her smile as she opened the front door for him. "Love you!"

"Love you too, Mum," Ty called over his shoulder with a matching smile, as he stepped off the porch.

* * *

Ty rounded the corner to the freshman hallway and couldn't help but smile. Further down the hall—his crew. His peeps. Lilith had on her skinny jeans, her sweater hung off one shoulder, and her light blond hair was up in a ponytail. She was laughing at something Serena was saying. Was that blue hair under the sequined beret Serena was wearing? He could have sworn she had pink hair the last time he saw her. There was no keeping up with that girl. Then there was Mylee...his favorite person in the world.

His smile faltered. Mylee's gorgeous long raven hair was down—just the way he liked it best—but she was doing that thing where she twirled a lock of it around her finger continuously. Something was bothering her. Worse yet, she had that forced, fake half smirk plastered on her face. This was bad. And she looked a little tired, too. Okay, this was bad in epic proportions. Time to get to work!

Slinging his backpack over one shoulder, he began an exaggerated runway strut. In his best imitation of Derek Zoolander, he cited some of his favorite movie dialogue. "Have you ever wondered if there was more to life, other than being really, really, ridiculously good looking? People come up to me all the time and say 'you should be a model,' or 'you look like a model,' or 'maybe you should try to be a man who models.'"

Ty had reached the girls at this point. He took a few steps beyond them in the hall and stopped, then swung around to face them again, flashing his best Magnum face. He continued in full Zoolander: "And I always have to laugh because...I'm so good looking. Of *course* I'm a model."

Lilith looked skeptical, but was holding back a laugh. Serena was rolling her eyes, shaking her head with an OMG-what-are-we-gonna-do-with-you?   expression on her face. Mylee—ah...there it was. A sincere, full-on smile and *YES!* A giggle! Was there anything more beautiful?

"'Mornin', ladies," Ty said with a smile.

"Morning, Ty," Mylee greeted. "Have a good weekend?"

"Not too bad. I got first place in a solo match in *Fortnite*."

"Daaaaang," Serena commented, clearly impressed.

Lilith nodded with raised eyebrows in agreement and added, "You da *man!*".

"Awesome! Way to go, Ty!" Mylee praised, flashing him another winning smile. Oh yeah. Breathtaking sunrises and double rainbows had nothing on this girl.

His attention was unfortunately distracted by someone approaching. Wait... what was this bozo doing in the freshman hallway?

"Hey, Mylee," said the worst part of his day with a cocky smirk.

"Sam...what are you doing in the freshman hallway?" quizzed a confused-sounding Serena.

"Just thought I'd check in with an old friend," he said, his eyes never leaving Mylee.

Mylee looked thoroughly confused. Lilith looked like she had just eaten some bad salmon. *See*, Ty thought, *it's unanimous. You aren't wanted here, Sam-a-lama-DING-DONG! Go back to your muscle-headed buddies and leave my crew alone!*

Mylee's lack of verbal response didn't deter Sam. "What? Don't you remember all the times we used to hang together?"

Mylee slowly shook her head no, with a continued deer-in-headlights expression.

"You know...at the park! Our moms used to get together all the time, talking about their old cheerleading days. They'd take us to the playground and we'd play together. I'd be showin' off my mad skills on the swings while you were kickin' it in the sand box."

Mylee finally spoke. "Oh, um...I guess we were pretty young. I don't remember that so much, but you're a few years older than me, so...I suppose it makes sense you'd have better memories from that long ago."

"Yeah, well...you *loved* it," Sam assured, as he casually propped himself against the lockers. "So, we have a game coming up Friday night, and I thought you'd probably enjoy a front-row seat to watch me and the rest of my bad-ass boys drive those wanna-be's from Bellevue into the ground. Whattaya say?" he asked as if it weren't a question so much as an announcement that she had just won the lottery or something. Ty suddenly felt like he had gotten some of Lilith's bad salmon.

Everyone turned their attention to Mylee, awaiting her response. Shaking herself out of her stupor, she quietly stammered, "Uh...sure? ...I guess." She ended with a shrug.

Noooooooo!!! What is she doing? She can't encourage this moron; he's all wrong for her! Ty bit the inside of his cheek to keep from voicing his objections.

"Perfect. Meet me at the fifty-yard line twenty minutes before the game. I'll show you your special V.I.P. reserved seat. I'll be the handsome guy with the big lucky number seven on his chest." Sam winked (*winked!*) and chuckled at his own wit and charm. He then turned his attention to acknowledge the rest of his audience. "Ladies," he said with a slight bow goodbye as he backed away, keeping his eyes trained on Ty after the obvious insult. Ty didn't give him the satisfaction, keeping his expression carefully neutral, despite the inferno of rage burning within him.

"OMG?! What was *that* all about?" squealed Serena as she grabbed Mylee's arm and bounced up and down excitedly. *Yeah.* Ty wanted to know, too. *What the heck was THAT all about?!*

"I have no idea," admitted Mylee.

Lilith sighed heavily. "I've gotta get to class," she muttered as she left without so much as a goodbye.

"What's up with her?" Serena quizzed, looking at their retreating friend.

"Beats me," Mylee and Ty answered in unison.

"Jinx!" all three exclaimed, then laughed.

The bell rang. "We'll discuss this awesome, exciting new development later, girlfriend!" Serena yelled as she jetted for class.

Ty walked alongside Mylee. "Hey...since I was so rudely interrupted by Mr. Football, I didn't get a chance to ask you about your weekend. At lunch I want to hear all about how things went with Grammy Jean. I know you were dreading the big move. I hope it went okay."

"Thanks, Ty," she said sincerely. "It went...as well as it could have, I guess. We can talk more later. Enjoy science!"

"And you have *una muy buena clase de español!*" he called over his shoulder as he broke away from her to head down a different hallway.

* * *

Making it to the cafeteria first, Ty staked out a claim at their usual table. Lilith was next to make her way over. She uncere-moniously threw her lunch tray onto the table and plopped herself down on the seat across from him.

"Hey," he greeted.

"Hey," she sighed, avoiding eye contact.

Nope. She wasn't over whatever had got-ten her all triggered earlier. He was saved from any further uncomfortable silence when Serena and Mylee showed up at the table together.

Serena hadn't even sat down before she started grilling Mylee. "Okay, so, like, *what's* with you and Mr. Hotty-McHot-Pants Football Star?! You never told me you knew him!"

"I don't, really. His mom and my mom know each other, but we didn't even go to the same school before this year. He must have gone to Franklin Middle School, because he wasn't at Lakeside."

"Hmmm...I had heard that he totally had a thing for the captain of the cheerleading squad—Olivia, I think her name is—but she's apparently been playing a big game of hard-to-get. Either I heard all wrong or he finally gave up on her. Anyway, you've clearly made some sort of impression on him in the month since school started, 'cause now here you are, goin' on a big date with him!" Serena rubbed her hands together excitedly.

"It's not a date," Ty, Mylee and Lilith all blurted out together.

"Not yet," Serena said in a sing-song voice as she opened her milk carton, "but I bet it'll turn into one."

Lilith gathered up her lunch tray. "Sorry, guys," she apologized quietly, continuing to look anywhere but at them. "I just remembered I need to meet with Mrs. Trahan about the coding assignment I missed in Tech class the other day."

"Okay," Serena mumbled around a carrot stick as she watched her friend walk away. "I seriously need to find out what's up with that girl."

Ty quickly changed the subject as he dug into his mac and cheese. "So, My, you were going to tell me how Grammy Jean is doing."

"She's okay. Her little apartment is cute and all—" She tipped her head from side to side, like she was trying to decide how best to answer. "—But...it's not *home*. And...I hadn't realized how much I'd miss her being *right there* for me, know what I mean?"

Ty and Serena nodded in understanding. "Remember, she's still close; she's just up the hill," Serena reminded her as she rubbed Mylee's back supportively.

"Yeah, you're right," Mylee begrudgingly agreed. "I feel so selfish making it about me. The retirement home is much safer for her. It was the right thing to do. I just already miss the way life used to be. I'll get used to it eventually, though." She offered a half smirk that Ty wasn't fooled by.

"You have no reason to feel selfish," Ty argued. "I don't know anyone more self-less and giving than you. This was a big change for you. You have every right to mourn the loss of the life you've always known. We're here for you, though; *that* hasn't changed."

"I know. You guys are the best," Mylee said, looking a little less stressed and marginally happier. "Hey, is Ben going to be able to give us a ride to practice today?"

"Yeah," Ty assured her. "He got that part-time job he was hoping for at Trader Joe's, but he scheduled himself for later in the evenings on Mondays and Wednesdays."

Serena hopped back into the conversation. "Oh; I almost forgot! On my way to History I saw a sign-up for people to come in next Saturday afternoon to work on Homecoming decorations. I was thinking it'd be fun if we all came in to help out. You guys game?"

"Sure," Mylee agreed. "I don't have anything else going on. You're right; it sounds fun! Ty? You on board?"

Trying to drop his voice a half-octave or so, Ty said, "Are you kidding me?" He sat up straighter in his chair and puffed his chest out. "I don't like to *brag* or anything, but I was known as Homecoming Decorator-In-Chief back at Franklin. I think I could rearrange my schedule a bit so that I might *selflessly* share some of my extensive expertise here." Continuing in an arrogantly authoritative tone, he quizzed, "What are we going with this year, ladies? A *Night of the Living Dead* theme? *Mortal Kombat*? *Zombie Apocalypse*?"

The girls laughed, just as he'd hoped. And of *course* he'd be there! An opportunity to hang with Mylee and the gang? He couldn't think of a better way to spend a Saturday afternoon!

"Awesome," Serena cheered. "I'll track Lilith down and make sure she's good to go, too. Then I'll sign us all up. Ooo... if we'll be seeing you on Saturday, that means you'll be able to dish on all the delicious details about your date at the game Friday night!" she said, excitedly grabbing Mylee's arm.

Ugh...Ty could have done without that little buzzkill. "It's not a *date!*" he and Mylee said, once again in perfect harmony. They all laughed, but inside Ty groaned, hoping beyond hope he and Mylee were right on their assessment of that stupid invitation to watch the stupid football game. It *couldn't* be a date!

* * *

Ty held open the back passenger-side door to his brother's beat-up red Toyota Corolla while Mylee climbed in. "Hey, Ben!" he heard Mylee greet in her sunniest voice, as he swung himself in next to her. She had bet Ty at the beginning of the year that she would get Ben to smile. Ty was looking forward to the homemade batch of chocolate chip cookies he knew he was going to win when she realized it was physically impossible for Ben to maneuver his face into any form of pleasant expression. He and his brother shared their tall, thin build, their sandy blond hair, and even their blue eyes. Their personalities were polar opposites, though, so the poor girl didn't stand a chance with this bet.

"Hey," his brother responded absently, as he flipped through radio stations. Funny how that one little three-letter word so easily translated to, "Listen. Giving you two a ride to practice twice a week is nothing more than a dreaded chore to me, one that I would never do, except Mum is *making* me. It's like some kind of sick and twisted punishment for living in the basement while I take my classes at the Tech. So, don't *push it* by expecting conversation."

"Don't mind him," Ty whisper-yelled for Ben's benefit. "He just started Chauffeur 101 and they haven't gotten to the unit on proper car conversation etiquette yet."

Ben answered by cranking up his classic rock tunes. Mylee and Ty shared a giggle.

Ten minutes later, they strode across the gym to join the rest of their team for tramp & tumble practice. "Okay!" Coach Tad demanded their attention. "Let's warm up with some straight jumps on the double-mini. Go!"

Mylee and Ty got in line for the warm-up jumps. "So, what's the deal with this sudden football game invitation from God's Gift to the Goal Line?" Ty quizzed, unable to hold back his irritated curiosity any longer.

"I really don't know," Mylee insisted. "I'm not even into football, so when he asked, I was wracking my brain about why the heck he was asking *me*. If I had been thinking, I would have come up with a way to politely turn him down. All of a sudden, though, everyone was staring at me, so I panicked and just said yes. Stupid, stupid, stupid. Now I have to sit through a *football* game." With that, Mylee turned and ran toward the double-mini for her first warm-up jump.

With effort, Ty refrained from pumping his fist in celebration. Mylee wasn't interested in Señor Jock Strap. Whew! He started running his pass as soon as Mylee had safely landed on the mat ahead of him.

"Now that I think about it..." Mylee continued as they made their way back to the end of the line, "...I'm actually worried that my mom was somehow involved with it."

"What would your mom have to do with a game invitation from Sam?"

"I don't know for sure, but it all just seems pretty suspicious. Yesterday she told me she had run into Sam's mom. Then she got all dreamy-eyed as she reminisced about 'the good ole days'." Mylee rolled her eyes and shook her head. "She specifically mentioned Sam, though. I didn't think much about it at the time; I figured she was just trying to talk me into cheerleading from some weird new angle." Mylee ran ahead for another pass.

"She's still hassling you about being on the T&T team, huh?" Ty quizzed after running his pass. "I kinda thought maybe she'd lay off a bit once it was too late for you to sign up for cheer."

"Okay," Coach Tad yelled out, "you can start with your double-mini passes and add in your tumbling pass."

"I thought so, too," Mylee said with a sigh. "I think she's finally given up on football cheer, but now she's pushing for *basketball* cheer." With that she ran to the double-mini, executing a flawless tuck jump, Barani (front somersault with a half twist), pike.

Ty loved watching Mylee flip. She was poetry in motion. After his double-mini mounter back tuck, Barani layout, he joined Mylee at the tumble track. She was just taking off for a round-off, triple back handspring, back tuck. He followed her with a round-off, quadruple back handspring, back layout.

Now they were starting to breathe a little heavier in line. "I don't get why your mom is so anti-T&T," Ty huffed.

"Nice layout, dude; you got some killer height on that one!" Mylee offered a high-five. "As for Mom, she loved cheer-leading, so she assumes I'd love it, too. More than that, though, I think she wants the *glory* of me on the squad. She doesn't consider tramp and tumble a "real" sport. She's all, 'What would you even do with T&T if you keep up with it? With cheer-leading, not only can you move on to college with it, you can be the envy of all the girls on campus and a shining star on the sidelines. You can even go pro! Who's even *heard* of tramp and tumble? Even if you found a college that offered it, it's not like you'd have fans lining up for the chance to watch you!'".

"Wow." Ty shook his head as he realized just how much Mylee was being hassled at home for participating in her sport of choice. It made him thankful for the support his parents gave him. Before he could respond further, Mylee was off on her next run. How could her mother not take Mylee's athletic achievements seriously? Not only had she made it to Regionals last spring, earning her an awesome trip to Las Vegas to compete, but she had gotten onto the podium in all three events, including a silver and a gold! His irritation at the disrespect for his friend's efforts made him over-rotate his double front tuck off the double-mini, setting him up for a perfect nose dive into the mat. He jumped up, yelling, "And he sticks the landing, ladies and gentlemen!" He looked over to Mylee in time to see he was responsible for yet another My-smile and giggle. Totally worth a crash and burn landing, anytime.

Chapter III

Mylee

A long, hot shower helped Mylee unwind after practice. She was feeling especially proud of the particularly clean Barani pike, straddle jump, back somersault tuck combo she did on the up tramp. Coach Tad had even smiled, clapped, and given her a high-five. He *never* did that!

She would have loved to share her special moment with her parents at dinner. She imagined announcing her accomplishment and Dad gushing, "Wow! Way to go, kiddo! That's *great!*" She pictured her mom running up and pulling her into a hug, whispering, "So, so *proud* of you!" It didn't work out that way, though. Things were more tense than usual around the table. It was enough to kill whatever appetite she had worked up at practice. Mom and Dad hardly said three words to each other, and neither seemed overly interested in chatting with Mylee, either.

She choked down a few bites of pot roast and, not being able to stand another minute of the awkward, uncomfortable silence, she got up to scrape the rest into the trash. She worried she'd get yelled at, told to get her butt back to the table and finish her dinner. Mom and Dad were too distracted, though; they didn't seem to notice she had even moved. As soon as her dishes were loaded in the dishwasher, Mylee quickly and quietly retreated to her bedroom.

Once homework was out of the way, she thought about going out to the living room to watch a little TV before bedtime. Opening her bedroom door, she found the cloud of tension hovering over Mom and Dad had moved with them from the dining room to the living room and had escalated to arguments...again. She quietly shut her door and padded back to her bed. She didn't know why she was making the effort to be quiet with her movements. Mom and Dad probably wouldn't have noticed if she had been right under their noses, singing show tunes. Well... Mom would notice if she went out and declared she was ready to quit T&T and try out for the cheerleading squad. She wasn't that desperate...yet.

She threw her head back onto her pillows with a frustrated sigh and grabbed her phone off the bedside table.

Text to Serena: Hey, chickee, whatcha up 2?

Serena: Drowning.

Mylee: What?!

Serena: Drowning in research 4 my History project. Ugh. U?

Mylee: Nothing. Just hangin'. I'll let u get back 2 it. Show dat research who's boss! ☺

Text to Ty: Dude! Wuzzup?

Ty: My! What's a girl like u doing on a phone like this?

Mylee: Wishing I was somewhere else.

Ty: Come on over, then! Fam n me r catching a few history lessons.

Mylee: What???

Ty: Binge-watching Drunk History. Learned more in 1 episode than I ever will from Mr. Harrow. Wanna join us?

Mylee: Nah. It's late & don't feel like approaching the parental unit for permission. Enjoy the show. TTYL

Ty: K. See u tomorrow! ☺

Text to Lilith: Hey, lady of few words... missed u today!

...[no response]...

Mylee: U kept disappearing. Everything ok?

...[no response]...

Mylee: I'll check in w/u in the morning. Have a great night! ☺

Well, that hadn't been nearly as distracting as she had hoped. Mylee set her phone back on the table, trying not to feel lonely and sorry for herself. Looking across the room, she caught sight of the box of Grammy's hand mirrors. She grabbed it and made her way back to her bed.

She took each mirror out of the box for a careful inspection. Who would have thought hand mirrors could be so varied? There were larger ones and smaller ones, wooden ones and velvet-covered ones. She was particularly fond of some of the intricate designs etched, carved, or embroidered into the backs of the mirrors. A pewter one looked really cool, with a winter scene depicted on the back. She put that one in her "keeper" pile, alongside the silver one that came with a matching brush.

Pulling up the final layer of newspaper, Mylee sucked in a startled breath. Sitting at the bottom of the box was the most beautifully crafted...anything...she had ever seen! The mirror looked to be made of pure gold that shone as if freshly polished. It must have taken years to work such minute details into the intricate floral design depicted in the precious metal. Making the entire scene "pop," making Mylee feel like she had, indeed, stepped into a gorgeous garden, surrounded by fragrant blooms and dancing butterflies, were jewels that the Queen of England would envy. They included sparkling diamonds, vivid emeralds, rubies of deep red, sapphires that shone so brightly they appeared to create their own illumination, and countless other shiny, colorful gems. All had been painstakingly shaped and placed to create a priceless piece of art.

With shaking hands Mylee gently lifted the mirror out of the box by the very edges. She couldn't bear the thought of marring the masterpiece with fingerprints. How could Grammy not have kept this beauty with her at all times? Maybe it was too valuable to leave out for anyone to see. Then, why wasn't it locked away in a vault...on a bed of velvet...in a glass case? How did it ever find its way to the bottom of a box, pushed to the back of an attic?

Carefully turning it over to see the glass of the actual mirror and any design that may continue on the front, she was startled into almost dropping it onto her bed. The glass was completely intact without so much as a scratch or smudge, surrounded by more of the gorgeous floral design. But it didn't...*work!* Or, at least, not the way mirrors are supposed to work. Mylee was holding it directly in front of her face. It should have been her pale green eyes, black hair, and bedroom wall she saw reflected back. That's not what the glass showed. Mylee found herself looking at a garden scene—one that very much resembled the design she had just admired on the back of the mirror—including an actual fluttering butterfly! How could that be? She quickly set it down on her bedside table...face down. Either she was a lot more tired than she had thought, or...well, she couldn't even think of any other explanation.

She quickly gathered up the rest of the mirrors, returned them to the box, and set them down on the floor. Then she climbed under her covers and shut her bedside light off. She refused to think any further about what she had just seen.

It wasn't too difficult to become distracted from the mirror mystery. Mom and Dad were now yelling louder than she had ever heard them yell at each other before. It was pretty hard to think about anything else. After a while she threw her pillow over her head, desperate to drown out the anger, frustration, accusations, and arguments assaulting her ears.

Sometime later—Mylee had no idea how long, but it felt like hours—the fight ended abruptly with the slamming of the front door. As frightened as she had been by what she had been hearing, she found the silence that followed to be infinitely more terrifying. She didn't dare leave her bedroom, afraid of what she'd find on the other side of her door. Wiping tears from her eyes and turning her pillow over to the dry side, she tried desperately to let sleep take her away from all her troubles. Sometime later—Mylee had no idea how long, but it felt like hours—sleep finally offered her escape.

* * *

The house remained eerily quiet the next morning as Mylee ventured out of the sanctuary of her room. She stumbled her way through throwing a slice of bread in the toaster and grabbing a glass of orange juice as she pondered strategies to stay awake in her Language Arts class. Her eyelids felt like they were lined with sandpaper and her thoughts seemed to be trudging through some sort of brain sludge. It would be a colossal challenge to remain conscious through Ms. Thaler's lecture on *Romeo and Juliet.*

As she spread peanut butter on her toast, Mom joined her in the kitchen, making a slow-but-determined shuffle toward the coffeemaker. Mylee hardly recognized her. Her hair was half falling out of a messy bun, and she had dark circles around her eyes. She wasn't even wearing any makeup! Mylee struggled to remember any time when Mom's makeup wasn't flawlessly applied long before she ever left her room. She didn't think Mom usually even left her *bed* without at least first applying a fresh coat of lipstick. And Mylee had never seen the "sloppy housewife" robe and slipper ensemble she now sported, either. Even when Mom had had the flu last winter she had always appeared the perfect picture of fashion. The only clue to her illness had been a slightly red nose.

Mylee also couldn't help but notice Dad wasn't joining them, grabbing his usual bagel with cream cheese to eat in the car on his way to work. "Where's Dad?" she asked, before her struggling brain could really think through the wisdom of that question or her interest in *really* knowing the answer.

"He...he has a meeting he had to go in early and prepare for," Mom mumbled. "He'll be back tonight...he'll...he'll be back," she repeated with a determined-looking nod, as if to reassure herself as she wandered back to her room, coffee mug in hand.

Mylee knew Mom wasn't being honest with her. There had been no mistaking the sound of Dad leaving the night before. Appetite disappearing with the realization that her family might be falling apart, she threw the rest of her toast in the trash, grabbed her backpack, and headed out to the bus stop.

* * *

"Well, hi, Babes!" Grammy exclaimed as she greeted Mylee at her little apartment door.

"Hi, Grammy," Mylee responded as she threw herself into a big hug with her grandmother. "It feels like forever since you moved over here. Are you settling in okay?"

"Yes, yes," Grammy assured her. "You're lucky you caught me, actually. I just got back from a big game of dominos. Last night it was canasta and the night before that was bingo. If I keep this pace up, I'll be all tuckered out by the end of the week!" she predicted with a chuckle.

"That's awesome, Grammy." Mylee smiled as she made her way to the sofa and Grammy plopped herself down in her recliner with a satisfied sigh. "It's so cool that they have all these activities here, so you can get to know your neighbors."

"Yes, well, it would appear my last few days have been significantly better than yours. You look terrible!"

"Gee, thanks!" Mylee tried to joke, but the laugh she was going for fizzed to a sad, soft puff of air.

Grammy waited patiently for Mylee to share whatever was obviously bothering her.

"Oh, Grammy." Mylee sighed, relieved to feel safe enough to share all her concerns. "You're right. It has been a tough couple of days. Mom and Dad are fighting again, and this time it's...different than before. Dad stormed out last night, and he wasn't home this morning. I don't know what's happening between them, but...it's bad, whatever it is."

"Honey, I'm so sorry. That must be heartbreaking for you to see and hear." She punctuated her condolences by leaning forward to lovingly pat Mylee's hand. "I don't know what's going on, either; your mom hasn't confided in me. Not much new there." Grammy shook her head. "Whatever it is, though, remember it has *nothing* to do with you. They may be trying to work through their own issues with each other, but one thing that will never change is that they both love you to the moon and back—just as I do. Give them some time, sweetheart. I'm sure it will all sort itself out."

"Okay. I'll try. And then there's all this ridiculous drama at school that I don't even understand," Mylee forged on, partly enjoying the opportunity to vent and partly desperate to move on from the scary and depressing subject of her parents. "It started yesterday morning when Sam, this big football guy that all the girls are apparently in love with. He invited me to watch his game on Friday. I was totally shocked by him even *talking* to me! I thought he was a stranger, but he claims we used to play together as kids because our moms are friends— *whatever*. Well, I ended up saying yes, because I couldn't think of anything else to say. Then Lilith stormed off in a huff and Serena was congratulating me for snagging Lakeview High's most eligible beefcake. I just shook it off, chalking it up to an upcoming wasted hour on an otherwise perfectly good Friday night. Football games don't last more than an hour, do they? Man, I sure hope not... Anyway, I got to school this morning, all stressed out about everything going on at home, and Lilith pulls me into the girls' bathroom to chew me out! *Apparently*, I stole the love of her life because I'm going on this *hot date* with Sam. You'd think I had chased him down and made him sign a marriage contract, the way she was accusing me! Yeah, right! I didn't even *know* him! And I certainly didn't ask for an invitation to some dumb football game! And—seriously—how the heck does that even qualify as a date, anyway? I tried to explain that if she's interested in Sam I am no threat to her. *Believe* me. Dating is the last thing on my mind right now! It was hard to convince her, though, when rumors about Sam and me were flying around school at the speed of light. By the end of the day, people were practically placing bets on what Sam and I will name our kids." Mylee's words tumbled over themselves as they rushed from her mouth. She punctuated her rant by sitting back on the sofa, crossing her arms angrily across her chest, and heaving a frustrated sigh that turned into an attempt to blow a few errant strands of hair from her eyes.

Mylee took a breath and prepared to continue to vent, because it had actually felt pretty danged good to get all that off her chest, but she was startled out of her tirade by the sound of Grammy's chuckle.

"Oh, honey, you've landed yourself in quite the little pickle, now, haven't you?"

Mylee wanted to hold on to her irritation and outrage for rant-round-two, but she so loved the sound of Grammy's laugh that a giggle of her own escaped and she couldn't seem to wipe the half smirk off her face. Besides...now that she had said it all out loud, the whole situation *did* seem rather silly.

"Oh, what tangled webs of love we weave! Oh! Sorry. I didn't mean to make that W-E-B reference. I know how sensitive you are about anything arachnid-associated."

Mylee nodded her head to let Grammy know it hadn't thrown her off...too much, as she concentrated on *not* imagining the terrifying and icky feeling of getting caught in a W. E. ...well, one of those.

"I'm sure Lilith will be back to acting like herself once she's had a few days to recognize the difference between the scenario she had built up in her mind about you and the boy and what has actually happened," Grammy continued.

"Be patient. She's a good friend and worth the wait. A high-school crush sometimes has a diminishing effect on brain power and common sense, but given a little time, they usually come back...accompanied by apologies for any friendships placed in jeopardy by the temporary insanity. As for anyone else spreading rumors, just try to let it roll off your back. Before you know it, some shiny new gossip will pop up and all those shallow little minds will chase after it like a starving pack of hounds, completely forgetting your little two-bit tale in the process."

"You really think so?"

"Of course; that's just run-of-the-mill high-school drama right there," she assured with a swipe of her hand, like she was shooing away the silly thought of it ever being anything more than that. "Everyone's all suddenly in a dither over something, then in the blink of an eye a new drama crops up and the first is completely forgotten. Don't you worry your pretty little head over it," Grammy advised. "Besides, it can't be so bad to have the attention of one of the most popular boys in school, can it?"

"Pfff...he's good looking and all, but I don't know what all the hub-bub is about. I've only spent five minutes with him—that I can remember, anyway—and the only impression I've gotten so far is that he's either trying to be funny, acting like an overly self-confident jock, or...he's a totally overly self-confident jock."

Grammy chuckled. "You are wise beyond your years, dear, to judge beyond physical appearance. It's what's in the heart that matters most."

"How is it that Mom grew up in your house? Appearance is *everything* to her! As a matter of fact, I think she somehow played a part in Sam suddenly talking to me, like maybe she and Sam's mom were playing matchmakers. It would be totally like Mom to think she was doing me some big favor by setting me up with the hottest guy in school. Oh, totally off subject, Grammy, but do you remember a particularly beautiful hand mirror in your collection?"

"Well, I saw beauty in all of them, sweetheart. Which one are you thinking of?"

"There's one I found at the bottom of the box that looked like it should be showcased at the Louvre or something. It's gold and is full of what looks like priceless gems, and the actual mirror part... seems like maybe it's a trick mirror or something?" Mylee's voice swung up to a questioning tone, as she really didn't know what happened the night before, much less how to describe it.

"Hmmm...I can't say as I remember a mirror that fits that description. Maybe you can bring it by so we can look at it together. Now, I have a favor to ask," Grammy announced with a determined tone. "I need to make some cookies and would love a hand. The girls and I decided to use baked goods as our currency in our poker game tomorrow. I plan on whippin' their butts, so maybe you can come back Thursday and help me eat all my winnings!"

"Sounds awesome." Mylee laughed as she helped Grammy out of her chair and skipped into the kitchen, feeling more herself than she had in days.

Two batches of chocolate chip cookies later—one for the card game and one for Mylee to share at her next T&T practice—and Mylee headed out to catch the bus home. Cooking in Grammy's new, smaller kitchen had felt a little strange, but more than that it felt really good to enjoy one of their favorite activities together. As she exited the building, she noticed a young girl posting a flyer on one of the porch columns.

"Hi." The girl smiled in a friendly greeting.

"Hi," Mylee returned, as she looked at the flyer. "What's this all about?"

"Oh, we're going to be selling dried flower arrangements at Big Finn Hill Park on Saturday to raise money for next year's seeds."

"Next year's seeds?"

"Yeah. Sorry, that probably sounds really weird." The girl laughed. "My name is D.J., by the way. I'm in a gardening club and we grew a bunch of veggies over the summer that we shared with the residents here. They seemed to really appreciate it, so we want to do it again next year, and we thought this would be a good way to make money for the seeds we'll need in the spring."

"Oh, cool! And I'm Mylee. My grandmother just moved here Sunday."

"Nice to meet you, Mylee. Maybe you'd be interested in stopping by the park on Saturday? Actually, it'll just be a bunch of us kids making flower arrangements and selling what we can; you're more than welcome to help us make up the bouquets, if you want. It's really fun."

Mylee read over the details on the flyer. "Hmmm... I have an event at the high school that afternoon, but it looks like this sale will be over in time for that. Yeah...I think I will join you. Grammy loves fresh vegetables, so it'd be cool if you came back next year, plus I think it'd be fun to play florist for a day!"

"Awesome! See you then." D.J. beamed. "If you'll excuse me, I'm headed inside to put another flyer on the bulletin board."

Mylee made her way to the bus stop feeling refreshed and ready to face life again.

Chapter IV

Mylee

Dad wasn't home when Mylee returned from her visit with Grammy Jean. Once again, the house was strangely quiet. Mom had moved from her bedroom to the couch in the living room, but she was still in the robe Mylee had seen her in that morning.

"Hey, Mom!" Mylee went with a cheery approach.

Mom turned from her blank stare at *The Ellen DeGeneres Show*. "Hi. How was your day?"

Mylee could tell Mom was trying to portray energy and interest with her query, but she was only pulling off fatigue and obligation. She appreciated the effort anyway. It had obviously been a rough day for her mom, and as irritated with her as Mylee had been lately, she felt bad for her and wanted to do what she could to cheer her up. "Fine. I ended up having some dinner with Grammy. Have you had anything yet? I can make you up some soup and a sandwich."

"Thanks, honey, but I'm not very hungry." Mom sat up a little straighter on the couch. "Hey!" she said, with the most spark and enthusiasm Mylee had seen from her all day. "I hear you have a date on Friday night!"

Mylee concentrated on holding in the sigh and eye roll that had become something of a natural reflex when talking with her mother. Mom needed love and support, not attitude. "No. No date. Just going to watch a football game."

"Oh! And is there any player in particular you'll be paying close attention to?" Mom pushed with a knowing grin and a raise of her eyebrow.

"No. Although, Sam Martin invited me, specifically. I have no idea whyyyy," Mylee dragged out the last word and shot an accusing glance at Mom.

"No idea why?" Mom repeated in a shocked tone. "Honey, you are absolutely gorgeous when you choose to dress with some thought and put yourself together with a little effort. It's no wonder the hottest guy in the school is interested in you," Mom complimented/nagged in the way she had perfected over the years. Clearly, she had missed Mylee's sarcasm, mistaking it for an ego that needed boosting... and criticizing.

"Are you saying you had nothing to do with Sam's out-of-the-blue invitation?"

"No," Mom said with a swipe of her hand.

Mylee waited, knowing Mom wouldn't leave it at that.

"I mean..." Mom continued, just as Mylee knew she would, "...of course I shared with Penny how proud I am of you..."

Mylee perked up, wondering what might follow those words. Was Mom appreciating the effort she was putting into tramp & tumble, despite her campaign to get Mylee to switch sports? Was she noticing how Mylee was keeping up with straight A's in her classes, despite the stressful transition from middle- to high school?

"...how beautiful you've grown up to be," Mom finished with a smile.

Beautiful?! What's to be proud of when it comes to physical appearance? It's not something Mylee was *working* on. Besides, did that mean that Mom *wouldn't* be proud of her if she had happened to suffer some tragic accident that left her scarred or disabled or unattractive in any other way? Mom looked on expectantly. Mylee knew she was looking for thanks to her compliment, but she just couldn't muster gratitude.

When Mom seemed to realize she wouldn't get the response she was seeking, she shook her head as if shaking off her disappointment. "So, of course Penny wanted to see some pictures—it had been years since she last saw you, after all—and I obliged, showing her some of the shots from that last photo session I arranged for you, the one you looked amazing in, no matter how much you fought me on doing it." It was Mom's turn to shoot an accusatory glance across the room.

Mylee took a calming breath, reminding herself she was *not* here to argue. She didn't know why her mother insisted on dolling her up once a year and placing her in all sorts of fake, magazine-ready poses, in clothes she would never normally wear, in locations that had probably been agonized over for months ahead of time. Those pictures weren't *her*. The person in those images was an imposter.

"Then Penny pulled out her phone, sharing some recent shots of Sam," Mom's words pulled Mylee from her reverie. "Oh, he is just totes adorbs, isn't he?"

"Ohmygod, Mom! *Nobody* says that anymore!" Mylee scolded, closing her eyes, shaking her head and pinching the bridge of her nose in embarrassment.

"Well he *is* a very handsome fellow," Mom gushed, apparently unphased by Mylee's reprimand. "I might have mentioned to Penny how amazing it would be if the two of you happened to get together. I didn't *really* think she would follow through and say anything to Sam! How lucky for you that she did, though, huh?"

"Yeah...lucky." Mylee shook her head as she turned for her room. Mom's mood seemed to have brightened. Mylee knew if she allowed the conversation to continue much longer they'd end up arguing. "If you need me, I'll be in my room. I have a ton of homework," she excused herself as she started walking down the hallway.

"We'll go through your closet tomorrow and see if you have anything acceptable to wear to the game on Friday," Mom yelled after her.

Mylee allowed herself the roll of her eyes she had been so careful to stifle earlier. Then she fished her phone out of her pocket, feeling the vibrating notification of an incoming text. It was Ty. She made herself comfortable on her bed before reading it.

Text from Ty: Hey, My, u doin ok? U seemed a little out of it & more than a little stressed today.

Mylee: I'm ok. Just tired. Been having trouble sleeping lately.

Ty: Anything I can help w/?

Mylee: Thnx, but no. Visited Grammy & made cookies w/ her. That helped.

Ty: ☺ Her world-famous chocolate chip?

Mylee: LOL the very 1's!

Ty: OMG, did u save me 1?

Mylee: Grammy's gotcha covered. She insisted we make a batch for me 2 take 2 practice tomorrow.

Ty: I think I have a new crush. Think she'd go out w/me?

Mylee: LOL Don't think she has time 4 dates. Her social schedule has really filled up since she moved.

Ty: Dang. The good ones r always taken.

Mylee: LOL U goofball!

Ty: Seriously, tho—if u need anything or want to talk, I'm here.

Mylee: Thx, Ty. That means a lot. We'll talk tomorrow.

Ty: K. TTYL

Mylee reached over to plug her phone in, and a glint of gold caught her eye. The hand mirror. Carefully picking it up from her bedside table, she took a moment to admire the design while she gathered the courage to take another look at the mirror side. After a few fortifying breaths, she slowly turned the mirror in her hand— and promptly threw it onto her bed!

She had been too startled to have the thought to turn it face-down this time, so she found herself still staring, wide-eyed at—not her reflection, not the garden she had seen the night before— but an insanely gorgeous blond, blue-eyed woman. Who was regarding Mylee curiously. And speaking! Mylee must have missed whatever the woman said, because she was now repeating herself with some apparent irritation over the necessity to do so.

"Hello, and who might you be?" the image in the mirror asked slowly, carefully enunciating each word as if speaking to someone who doesn't speak English.

"Mylee," she answered in a near-whisper.

"Well, Mylee, care to share with me why you are in possession of my mirror?"

"Uhhh...it...it's your mirror? I didn't know. I—I mean, I found it. Well, I didn't, really.

My grandmother did...for her collection. It was at the bottom of the box. Grammy said she got most of the mirrors at yard and garage sales years ago; I'm sure she'd never take one without paying for it. Maybe...maybe it was put in a yard sale by mistake?" Mylee rambled nervously. The more she said, though, the darker the woman's mood seemed to grow, having progressed from a light mixture of amusement and slight irritation to positively dark and foreboding. Mylee was amazed that, even when apparently furious, the woman remained the picture of beauty personified.

Mylee zipped her lips closed, assuming if she went on any longer, the woman would get angrier and might just reach through the mirror to strangle her. Surely it would be gorgeous, perfectly manicured hands that would do the job, but it wouldn't be a pleasant experience, no matter how stunning the weapons were.

"Hermes!" the woman's image thundered, red-faced.

"Ummm...I'm not sure what you mean by that, but whatever is wrong, I'm sure we can work it out. If you just tell me where to take your mirror, I'll gladly return it to you!" Mylee sputtered fretfully as she silently planned an escape route, now fearing the woman would climb completely out of the mirror with a full-body attack.

"Oh, this will be worked out, for sure," the woman said with lethal conviction. "You must help me devise a plan of perfect revenge. Hermes will *pay* for hiding my mirror from me!"

Mylee didn't know who this Hermes guy was, but the woman was asking for her help, so she assumed that meant she wasn't accusing Mylee of being in league with him. That was good, because it seemed getting on this woman's bad side would be a monumentally bad idea. She took a calming breath and picked the mirror up off the bed, looking directly into it. "I'd love to help you if I can," she assured. "Would you mind sharing what happened? That might give me a better idea what I can do to best help you."

"Sure," the woman said with a shake of her head and deep, calming breath.

"Hermes—the Messenger God," she added with a dismissive swipe of her hand, "is a real pain in my a—" She stopped, closing her eyes as she appeared to take another moment to center herself. "A real prankster," she amended.

Mylee didn't know what to think. This woman was going on as if it were perfectly natural and normal to be talking about a god like some guy...some guy who had just royally ticked her off. Was she crazy? Although...this conversation *was* taking place *through a mirror*, so...crazy appeared to be the special on today's menu. Why not just run with it and leave the thinking for later? "Sorry," she rushed to sneak in, hoping her interruption wouldn't be perceived as rude, "but...do you mean Hermes, as in one of the Greek gods? I think we learned about them in our sixth-grade history class."

"Then you may be familiar with me, too. I'm Aphrodite."

Mylee gasped. "As in...the goddess of love?"

"Love *and beauty*," Aphrodite corrected, as she casually ran a hand through her luxurious golden hair.

"Oh. My. God!"

"Exactly, darling," the goddess pointed out with a wink.

"Oh." Mylee chuckled nervously. "Right. So, Hermes stole your mirror as a prank?"

"It's the only explanation. And what a clever little thief to hide it at the bottom of a random box of mirrors!"

"The mirror is very special to you, then?"

"What? No!" she scoffed with a scowl and a quick shake of her head. "It was just one of the many, many gifts Hephaestus made for me."

"Hifa-what-now?"

Aphrodite slowly sounded out the word. "Hi-*fes*-tus. My husband," she clarified with a roll of her eyes and a disgusted expression. "Even his name is awkward and strange," she added under her breath.

"Oh! Sorry, I...I guess I don't remember learning about you being married."

Mylee struggled to recall her lessons on the Greek gods.

"Trust me, darling; I'm not in the habit of bringing him up. Frankly, I tend to forget about him every chance I get." Aphrodite grinned like the Cheshire Cat.

Mylee's heart sank a bit, as she was reminded of the troubles her parents were having in their marriage. "I'm sorry to hear about your marital problems. I hope you'll be able to work it out," she quietly consoled.

"Think nothing of it; I certainly don't." At Mylee's uncomfortable, yet curious expression, Aphrodite continued. "Let's just say it was an arranged marriage— not that I would ever complain about any decision Zeus made," she rushed to add, looking up with a slight grimace as if half-expecting to be struck down by something.

"Wait. Zeus, himself, arranged your marriage?"

"Yes." Aphrodite sighed. "*Apparently* I was causing too much disruption because all the gods were fighting over me. I, personally, don't think it was as bad as all that. Sure, there was the occasional skirmish—or war, or whatever—but, honestly...those were some of the best days of my life! I'm sure everything would have worked out fine if all been allowed to progress naturally. But, oh no. Zeus had to stick his nose in my business, and instead of just *asking* me to tone down my magnetic attraction a bit—although, let's face it, that would have essentially been asking the impossible—he *decided* I would marry the lame metalworking god, Hephaestus, so he wouldn't have to hear any more arguing from the many gods vying for my attention!" She sighed heavily, as if relieved to have had the opportunity to vent.

"You said, though, that this mirror was a gift from Hephaestus. It's *so* beautiful! With the extensive time and effort he must have poured into it, I would guess he truly has feeling for you," Mylee ventured.

"Well, of course he does; who could blame him? And as the loving, caring, generous goddess I am, I make *every* effort to put up with him—his constant fawning over me, his endless stream of gifts, his unceasing declarations of love and devotion. It's just difficult to do when he was *foisted* upon me the way he was. The struggle is real," Aphrodite concluded with a dramatic sigh and slow shake of her head.

Mylee was beginning to feel over-whelmed. She tried to boil everything down to the essential facts. "Wow. Okay, so...your husband gave you this mirror. It's not particularly important to you, but you're angry with Hermes for hiding it on you, and you want revenge?"

"Yes, darling. However—" Aphrodite paused for a moment, looked up and to the left, and tapped her bottom lip with her finger, as if in contemplation. "Nothing that would kill or maim him, I think. He's rather easy on the eyes. Not Ares-level gorgeous, of course, but handsome enough that I believe I might miss the attractive view I presently enjoy when I look his way, should it be taken from me."

Whew! Mylee was thankful that at least she wasn't expected to mastermind a homicide...of a god, no less. Would that be godicide? "Got it," she assured. "A crushing blow of revenge that falls just shy of physical harm."

"Yes, exactly," Aphrodite encouraged. "What do you think? Do you have a plan?"

"Umm...nothing off the top of my head," Mylee ventured, hoping the admission wouldn't rekindle the goddess's anger.

"Well, you would, of course, endeavor to present me nothing less than the *perfect* plot. And with your mere mortal mind, that could take some time. So be it. I will allow you a bit of time to devise our scheme. Return to me in twenty-four hours," Aphrodite commanded.

Mylee nearly laughed out loud in fear and disbelief. No pressure! "Sure," she agreed with reluctance, "I'll...I'll work on that first thing tomorrow. You know what they say. Revenge is always best planned after a good night's sleep."

"Tomorrow, then," the goddess confirmed. "Good night, Mylee. And do get some sleep, darling. You have some very unfortunate dark bags under those eyes of yours."

With that, the view in the mirror briefly went out of focus, then reverted to the view of the garden. Mylee carefully set the mirror back on her bedside table. She couldn't believe what had just transpired. She feared if she told anyone about it, they'd assume she was crazy. Maybe she was. Maybe with the combination of Grammy moving, Mom and Dad fighting, the latest social drama at school, and her recent lack of sleep, she had finally cracked.

Fallen off the edge.

Best to keep the incident to herself. Maybe after some rest things would look and feel different in the morning.

Chapter V

Ty

Steam hung heavy in the locker room as Ty searched for Austin Miller. It was near the end of third period, Ty's study hall, and he had signed up to help in the office. Austin's mom stopped by to drop off a notebook Austin had forgotten at home, but would need for fourth period, and Ty volunteered to deliver it to him.

Ty found his mark sitting on a bench between the last two rows of lockers, tying his shoes as he prepared to head to his next class. "Ah, dude! Thanks," Austin exclaimed, looking very relieved. "Didn't know if Mom would come through for me, but she got it here just in the nick of time! Ms. Morris would have busted my butt if I showed up to class without my homework three days in a row!"

"Ms. Morris? Yikes! That woman could do some *serious* damage, too!" Ty chuckled in commiseration as he turned to leave. Remembering to bring his homework to school was often a challenge for him, as well. It wasn't as hard as remembering to *do* the homework, but he could certainly relate to the situation Austin found himself in. This was yet another reason homework needed to be outlawed. Nobody should be held responsible for all that thinking and remembering. If teachers wanted the work to be done, they should just have it done *in school* where work was meant to be done!

Just as he was nearing the double doors that exited back to the gym, a familiar, patronizing voice called out, "Oh, sweetheart; I think you've gotten lost. The girls' locker room is on the *other* side of the gym."

Ty looked over in the direction of the insult to find Sam smiling directly at him while elbowing one of his teammates in the ribs, apparently looking for either a laugh or back-up, should the situation come to blows. Seeing how all three of the football players Ty was now facing looked like they snorted steroids every morning for breakfast, he assumed none would see him as a threat, so it must have been the laugh Sam was looking for. Ty decided to give him one.

Bending over and wrapping his arms around his abdomen, he barked out a loud, fake laugh. Rising back up to a standing position, he wiped imaginary tears from his eyes. "Oh! That was a good one, Sam! Whew!" He panted, as if catching his breath. "Did you stay—up all night—formulating that burn—or are you just naturally talented at slinging slights?"

"Pff..." was Sam's sorry excuse for a snappy comeback. After an awkward beat of silence, he tried to recover the upper hand in the verbal sparring match. "I'll be staying up all night, for sure...Friday after the game with hot little Mylee keeping me company!" He crossed his arms across his chest in a satisfied stance and smiled, as if he had just scored a point.

Ty didn't want to give Sam the satisfaction of responding in anger, knowing that was exactly what the testosterone twit wanted. That was an immense challenge, as he was seeing red at the thought of his Mylee being harmed, defamed, or taken advantage of in any way. He miraculously limited his explosive outburst to a slight narrowing of his eyes and clenching of his teeth. After all, this had to be Sam just goading him, right? Mylee had no interest in even going to the game. She might even leave the game early, much less stay to do anything with Sam afterward. Right?

Keeping his rage over Sam's sick insinuation bottled up, Ty couldn't help himself from poking at the beast by declaring his territory. "All night? In your dreams! She'll suffer through a few hours of your game, then she'll come right back to me and tell me all about how she was reminded just how much she hates football."

"Oh, that's right. You're one of her *besties*. Well, Tinkerbell, while you're stuck in the *friend zone*, I'll be dancing in the end zone. Not only will I blow her mind on Friday, but I'll be rockin' her world at Homecoming, too."

Ty was too stunned to speak. Mylee was going to the Homecoming dance with Sam? When did *that* happen?!

Sam must have caught Ty's astonishment, because he turned to his sidekicks and laughed. "Oh, guys; can you believe this? Little Freshman Friend Zone Freddy over here thought he had a chance with Mylee!" Turning his attention back to Ty he sneered, "Did you honestly think you had anything that could compete with a Friday night date with the captain of the football team, then walking into the Homecoming dance on the arm of Homecoming King? I guarantee she'll be putty in my hands in no time. And believe me. I can't *wait* to get my hands on her!"

Ty didn't know what he felt most: furious over the disgusting "plan" Sam had for Mylee?—or petrified over the prospect of Mylee actually falling for this Neanderthal?

It was such an overwhelming storm of emotion that he felt like he had been chewed up and spit into a puddle on the floor. Mustering every bit of dignity, too freaked out to worry about formulating a clever comeback, he simply shook his head and quietly said, "Shows how little you know Mylee."

With that, he was saved by the bell—the bell to end third period, that is. Before things could get any worse, he simply spun around, walked out of the locker room and headed to fourth period. He couldn't believe he had to sit through an entire Algebra class before he'd be able to talk to Mylee at lunch.

* * *

The forced time out ended up being helpful. Ty didn't catch too much about the quadratic equation Mr. Bretz was going on about with far too much excitement and enthusiasm, but he did take the opportunity to piece his fragmented brain back together.

Part of him wanted to hide Mylee away so Sam couldn't hurt her. Part of him wanted to thrash on Sam—after tranquilizing him first, of course, so he could ever stand a chance against him—for even uttering such disgusting and disrespectful words about *any* girl, but especially Mylee. Part of him wanted to scream at her for ever agreeing to go to the Homecoming dance with Sam. Part of him wanted to kick himself for never having the courage to ask Mylee out himself.

At the same time, part of him wanted to hug Mylee close and absorb whatever pain was dragging her down. He didn't know what was bothering her—well, besides Grammy Jean's move across town—but something was deeply upsetting her. She hadn't been herself all week, but today she had arrived at school not only just as sapped and stressed looking as she did yesterday, but also rather freaked out about something, too. Part of him wanted to just magically go back in time and enjoy the Las Vegas Regionals Tramp & Tumble meet with Mylee all over again. And part of him wanted to sneak into Ben's bathroom and replace his stick of deodorant with cream cheese. Because...that would just be *awesome*.

By the end of class, he decided he had to give Mylee a chance to tell him about the

Homecoming dance herself. He also had to have faith in her—in her decisions and her strength. He had to be gentle with whatever he did or said, though, knowing she was currently feeling rather fragile. He had to be patient with her, too. Pushing her about anything wouldn't be helpful, and helping her was all he wanted to do.

He sat down at the lunch table feeling quite Zen and chill. Then all hell broke loose. First Serena came over to the table squealing with delight over something. Before she had a chance to explain, Mylee walked over from the other side of the cafeteria. Serena dropped her lunch tray on the table and ran to Mylee, giving her a huge hug.

"Ohmygod, I just heard the news! I can't *believe* it! I'm soooo happy for you...and a little jealous, but that's okay. Tell me everything. I want to hear *every* detail! I may never have a fairytale moment like this, so I'll just live vicariously through you!" Serena was talking a mile a minute and practically vibrating with excitement.

Mylee looked thoroughly confused, but before she got a chance to question Serena, Lilith stormed over, threw her tray on the table, spun around to Mylee and Serena, and seethed, "How *could* you?!"

Ty wasn't quite sure whether she was addressing Mylee or Serena. By the looks on their faces, they didn't seem to know, either.

"How could we what?" Serena ventured.

"Not *we*. *You!*" Lilith yelled, pointing at Mylee. She was now shaking, and tears were welling in her eyes.

"I don't understand," Mylee said. "I don't know what I did. Whatever it was, I'm sorry. I wouldn't ever intentionally do anything to make you feel bad," she soothed.

"No. You don't even have to try, do you?" Lilith bit back. "You just flounce your way through life throwing that *perfect* hair around, batting those *perfect* eyes, and smiling that *perfect* smile; and the boys just fall all over you."

"What?! No, they—Lil, I don't understand. What are you talking about?"

"Oh, *puh-leez*! You know exactly what I'm talking about! You were so convincing the other day, too," Lilith said with a bitter laugh and shake of her head, "telling me you weren't interested in Sam, that you wouldn't do anything to get in my way of trying to date him, that you *respected* me as a friend too much to let some boy come between us!" Tears were streaming down Lilith's face, leaving behind two little faint black mascara tracks.

"And I meant every word I said!"

Ty felt like he was at a tennis match, his head was whipping back and forth between the girls so fast.

"Then why would you go behind my back and agree to go to *Homecoming* with Sam?! You know what? I don't even want to hear any more of your lies." Lilith grabbed her tray, dumped her entire lunch in the trash—a shame, because it was a chicken-nugget-and-French-fries day, and Ty could have totally taken those off her hands—then returned the tray to the kitchen on her way out.

"*Homecoming?* I didn't agree to go to Homecoming with anyone. I thought we were all going to go together," Mylee said to nobody in particular, looking thoroughly confused.

"Yes, you did," Serena contradicted. "Addison Clark texted me about it in Health class, who said she saw it on an Instagram post from Sarah Adams, who's dating one of Sam's linemen; so she's a pretty good source. And I don't know how to feel right now because I'm super excited for you, but I didn't know Lil felt that way about Sam! Although... with those hurtful things she just spat at you, I'm not really sure I know how I feel about Lilith anymore, either."

"Well, now you have an even better source," Mylee said, anger spilling forth in her tone. "Listen closely. I never told Sam I'd go to Homecoming with him!"

Ty nearly fell off his chair in relief.

"Well we're in the Twilight Zone, then, because your name has already been added to the ballot for Homecoming Queen," Serena assured Mylee. "I've even gone on Facebook and cast my vote! And if you go with Sam, you're practically a shoo-in for the title! Are you sure you didn't talk to Sam about Homecoming? Maybe you were distracted and agreed without knowing it, like when I ask my mom if it's okay to take twenty dollars out of her purse when she's in the middle of typing an email and she just gives me the I'm-not-really-listening-to-you-but-I-don't-want-to-be-a-bad-mom-and-seem-like-I'm-ignoring-you 'M-hmm'?"

"No. I think I'd remember talking with Sam about going to Homecoming!"

"Well, who cares how we got here, anyway? My! Think about it! The hottest, most popular guy in the whole high school—maybe even in the entire history of the high school—is apparently taking you—a mere freshman—to Homecoming! I can see it now: You're going to be the most stunning Homecoming King and Queen to ever grace the stage! So romantic!" Serena was on a roll.

Ty wanted to shove a dinner roll in her mouth. Before he could say anything, though, the devil, himself, sauntered over to their table. "Mylee! Can I talk to you for a minute?" Without waiting for a response, Sam pulled Mylee by the arm over to a corner and began quietly talking with her.

What was Sam saying? Why hadn't Mylee slapped him across the face yet? Her knee was *perfectly* poised to do some serious harm to his groin. Why wasn't Sam doubled over in pain yet? Every passing second felt like an eternity, and Ty didn't know how many more torturous ticks of the clock he could take. Then the situation got even worse. The bell rang. Lunch was over. Sam was walking out of the cafeteria, still in deep conversation with Mylee, and Ty hadn't had the chance to say a single word to her.

* * *

Ty held open the passenger-side rear door of his brother's car for Mylee. As he climbed in behind her, he heard her exclaim, "Ben! Did you do something new with your hair? It's looking absolutely *amazing* today!"

"Nope," was the monotone response she got before Ben reached over and cranked up his tunes.

"Better luck next time," Ty consoled with a chuckle, knowing she was never going to get Ben to crack a smile. "You remember I like walnuts in my cookies, right? Just want to make sure you'll be all prepared for when I win this bet."

Mylee playfully punched him in the arm, and they both laughed.

They had barely entered the gym before their teammate, Keelie, ran over to greet them. "Mylee! I just heard your Homecoming news! Congratulations!"

"What?!" Ty was incredulous. "You don't even go to our school!"

"Sheesh, Ty." Keelie rolled her eyes. "What are you, from the Dark Ages? Uh, there's this little thing called the *internet?*" She focused her attention back on Mylee. "I heard it on Snapchat, got confirmation on Twitter, and cast my vote for you on Facebook on my way over here. I don't know if my vote will count or not, but it was worth a shot! This is so exciting!" She jumped up and down, clapping her hands.

Coach Tad was calling them over for warm-ups. Ty thought Mylee had ample time to set Keelie straight as they made their way over to the up tramps, but she didn't take the opportunity. Why wasn't she clearing up this obvious case of misinformation? Frustration grew through warm-ups. Unlike Monday's practice, where they had time to chat while waiting in line at the double-mini, there was no time to talk here. Every time he was up on a trampoline, Mylee was either jumping on the other one or waiting her turn below.

By the time they got to the tumble track and Ty finally had a chance to ask Mylee what was going on, she shook her head, and with a sad, tired sigh, just said, "It's too much to explain right now. I'll try to call you tonight, and if I can't, I promise to talk to you tomorrow."

Taking a deep breath, he remembered back to his Algebra-class meditation session, reviewing his vow to be patient and understanding with Mylee, and to have faith in her and be there to support her however she wanted. They had had fun joking around in the car; he now wished he hadn't wasted that time. He should have spent the drive quizzing her about everything. But maybe a few light laughs had been just what she had needed. It was too late now. He wasn't going to push her. It was one of the hardest things he had ever done, but he managed to choke out, "No worries. Whatever works best for you," with a forced smile.

"Thanks, Ty," Mylee said with genuine gratitude. "You're the best friend a girl could ever have!" She offered him a quick hug, then was off, flipping through her tumbling pass. Ty placed his hand over the heart that felt like it was ripping out of his chest. The phrase "best friend ever" should be featured on the first page in the Big Book of Most Deadly Words Uttered By Girls. In huge, bold font with asterisks and warning labels all over it. There should be mandatory daily homework about it for girls, to avoid any unfortunate deaths by way of broken hearts.

* * *

"Hey, Buddy. Mind if I come in for a minute?" Mum knocked lightly on the door.

"Nope."

Mum stuck her head in the room and looked down to where the floor was once upon a time, presumably navigating a possible route to a spot where it might be safe to stand. Two small hops over piles of comic books to the left, then a long leap over a stack of foam *Overwatch* weapons to the right brought her to the foot of Ty's bed. Sliding a box of *Magic: The Gathering* cards off to one side and tossing a few *Star Wars* figures into the laundry basket sitting on his desk chair, she cautiously sat next to him on the bed and smiled. "Just wanted to check in with you," she said. "You seemed a bit off at dinner."

"I'm okay," Ty said in a tone even he could tell was anything but okay.

"Wanna talk about it?" she asked gently, absently pulling pug hairs from his blanket.

"Just a rough day at school." Ty sighed heavily, trying to figure out how much he wanted to share with Mum. "It's just..." He sighed one more time, then decided to just go for it. "Mylee is my favorite person in the whole world. No offense," he quickly added, "you're totally rockin' the number two spot. And it's *close*. So, so close."

"I appreciate that, buddy. You're definitely in my top ten," she teased.

"We've been best buds since fourth grade. Even though we weren't in the same schools, we at least always had our practices together and our meets. I thought going to the same school this year would be the best thing ever because we'd have even more time together. But...it's not working out the way I imagined."

"How so?"

"We used to hang out and it was just... fun, you know? It was so easy—laughing and having a good time. But now that we spend more time together, I'm starting to think it would be awesome to be more than just friends. But in *that* way, she's way out of my league. I mean...the freakin' *captain of the football team* wants to date her! Can you get any more '80s after-school special than that? I'm just the geeky sidekick friend. He's the starring role that all the girls drool over. I don't stand a chance!"

"Okay, let's break this all down," Mum said in her usual logical manner. "And bear with me; I'm about to go into some uncharted metaphor territory. Try to think of relationships in terms of architectural projects—like the Great Pyramids. To have any hope of building a pyramid what do you need?"

"Uh...slaves?"

Mum laughed. "No. Ugh...Tyler Alexander Davis, would you work with me here?! You need a strong *foundation!* Not every pyramid you set out to build will reach the sky and be worthy of listing as one of the Seven Wonders of the World.

But," she emphasized, "to have *any* hope of getting to that point, you need a really strong foundation. If you don't have that, your pyramid is just going to crumble and fall—*Every. Single. Time.* And nothing builds a stronger relationship foundation than a close friendship. *That's* what you and Mylee have, buddy." Mum paused, looking Ty in the eye. "No matter what other relationship pyramids either of you set out to build throughout your lives with other people, you'll *always* have that good solid base that you can either continue to build upon or come back to visit at any time. Sure, I had a few boyfriends through high school..."

"TMI, Mum, TMI!" Ty interrupted, shaking his head vigorously.

"I'll spare you the details, then," she chuckled. "The point is, I can barely remember any of their names. They were just...I don't know...sandcastles. They were fun for a little while, but they all quickly melted away. You'll probably have some of those in your life, too. They aren't a bad thing, necessarily—just nothing that is ever going to amount to anything.

"Anyway, all that stuff you were just spouting about 'not being able to compete' and being 'out of her league'? *Total* nonsense. You and Mylee share something that the football player will almost certainly *never* have with her—regardless of what their *relationship status*' might get changed to on Facebook in the short term."

"So, it's like angling to play the long game?"

"Yeah, you could say that. Out of curiosity, how do you know he wants to date her?"

"He says he *can't wait* to get his 'hands on her'—his words, not mine."

"Eww. Okay, he sounds like a total predator. I don't know Mylee as well as you do, but from what I do know of her, I can't imagine she'd be attracted to any type of attitude like *that*."

"I guess you're right. She just doesn't seem like herself lately, and I'm worried about her."

"Then be there for her as the awesome supportive friend you are."

"I'll try. Thanks, Mum."

"Anytime. Actually, you could repay me by cleaning your room up." At Ty's wide, panicked eyes, she amended, "Not even clean, really. A path. A path is all I ask for. Maybe one that leads to the window, so I can open it when the stank starts getting to a critical level in here?"

"I'll see what I can do."

Chapter VI

Mylee

"What do you have for me?" Aphrodite asked without preamble when Mylee raised the mirror to her face.

"Ummm...does Hermes have something that's really important to him?"

"Well, there's his talaria—that's those winged sandals he insists upon wearing, no matter how many times I tell him they're dreadfully out of style."

"Hmmm...he probably wears those all the time, though, right? Is there anything he cares about that would ever be out of his sight? It wouldn't have to be for long— just a minute or two."

"I suppose that would be his caduceus. That's a staff. It has two entwined snakes on it and wings at the top."

"And it's really important to him?"

"Oh yes. He's just as attached to it as he is to his talaria, but he is willing to put it down briefly, should he need the use of both of his hands."

"Perfect." Mylee smiled. "Do you think Hephaestus would be willing to help you?"

"Of course, darling. There's nothing he wouldn't do for me."

"Okay." Mylee took a cleansing breath, hoping Aphrodite would go for her idea. Actually, she wouldn't even have to agree to it. As long as she didn't explode in anger, Mylee would count this a win. "I was thinking you could ask Hephaestus to make a staff that looks identical to the one Hermes carries. Then, when Hermes sets his down, you can swap his for the fake one. After that, you can confront him about discovering his prank involving this mirror. With all the rage you probably legitimately feel on the matter, you can grab the fake staff and dramatically snap it in two right in front of him. Then you can sit back and enjoy his reaction until you're ready to let him know his real staff is safe and sound. Nobody gets hurt, nothing important gets damaged, and he'll sweat the loss for as long as you want." She held her breath, awaiting the verdict. She was holding it longer than she wanted, because Aphrodite just stared at her with no discernable emotion expressed on her beautiful face.

Finally, Aphrodite ended Mylee's suffering. "I do believe that could work," she said with a slow smile that dripped with evil intention spreading across her face. "Yes. That will do nicely."

Mylee sagged with relief. "That's good, because with the day I've had, I really needed something to go right."

"Having troubles, darling? I notice you didn't take my advice on getting sleep. I wouldn't have guessed you could look worse than last night, but, well...here we are."

Mylee didn't know what to do with Aphrodite's blunt assessment. She wasn't wrong, though. Mylee was feeling even more strung out and frazzled than she probably looked. "I'm 'in a pickle', as

Grammy Jean would say. My mom told me earlier this evening that she and Dad are 'on a break'. He's in an apartment across town. Seems to me that if it were just a 'break', he'd be in a hotel room or on a friend's couch, but maybe that's just me." Mylee expelled a frustrated sigh. "Mom is not taking this well, either. She's a total mess."

"*Worse* than you?" Aphrodite interrupted, apparently stunned at the thought.

"Much. She and I don't always get along, but I actually feel really bad for her. And that's making it hard for me because there's this boy at school, Sam—"

"Tell me about this Sam," the goddess demanded, eyes lighting up with interest.

"Well, he's the most popular boy at school, all the girls are in love with him, he's captain of the football team—"

"And you need him to fall in love with you. I can help you there, darling. You just need to don my golden belt, and he will find you simply irresistible...baggy, tired eyes and all."

"You have a belt that makes you irresistible to people? Not to be rude, but...isn't that overkill? You're already so gorgeous!"

"Yes, well, it is one of the more perplexing gifts from my husband. He was already head over heels for me, of course, so it certainly wasn't for his benefit. Why he would want me even more irresistible to others, I have no idea, but as it is one of my favorite gifts to play with, I've never questioned him on it," Aphrodite explained with a sly smile.

"Oh. Thank you, but no. Sam appears to be interested in me already...bizarre as that may be. I don't even know him, but somehow, he got it in his head to ask me to our Homecoming dance next week-end. Had he actually *asked* me, I probably would have passed. I want to go and have fun with the friends I know and love, so I can relax and be myself. I don't want to be constantly wondering and worrying about a virtual stranger as my date, no matter how popular or good looking he might be.

"Unfortunately, a rumor got started when Sam told a few of his teammates he planned to *take* me—not planned to *ask* me, mind you, but to *take* me to Homecoming. That spread faster than wildfire, so my good friend Lilith heard about it even before I did. She thinks she's in love with him, so she was livid with me, thinking I had agreed to the date. She yelled at me, accusing me of manipulating guys with my looks or something. Sam apologized to me for the 'unconventional invitation'. He was pretty sweet about it, actually. It was almost like he was a completely different person when we were alone than he was in front of my friends. He was so nice, in fact, I felt bad telling him no—especially when that would be embarrassing for him when the whole school thinks we're *a thing.*

"It still didn't feel right, though, and I was still really upset about Lilith being so mad at me, so I told him I would think about it. I planned on coming home and trying to find a great excuse for not going with him or the nicest way to turn him down, but as soon as I walked through the door after practice, Mom practically bowled me over in her excitement. The 'Date Heard Round the World' had already made its way to her, of course. And after all her screaming in delight she said, 'Mylee, things have been really rough lately, but hearing that you'll be going to Homecoming with Sam has made me happier than I've been in months. I can't wait to go gown shopping with you, and shoe shopping... Oh, and we can get our hair and nails done together. We'll make a total day of it!' Then she proceeded to hug me and actually *cry* with joy. She cried! How can I turn Sam down now? It would crush her!"

Aphrodite continued to stare at Mylee with a beautifully blank expression. Finally, with a quick shake of her head and a few blinks of her eyes, she broke the silence. "Oh, you're done? I'm still waiting for the problem. Sounds like not only are you going to the dance with the most popular guy at the school, but you've also weeded out an imposter friend because she never would have said hurtful things to you if she truly cared. Trust me, it happens to me all the time. On top of that, you've managed to make your mother happy. Um...win, win, and win! Get some sleep. Clearly your brain is as addled as you look. You'll surely see reason in the morning. Check in with me tomorrow; I'm intrigued. I want to hear more about Sam. Goodnight, darling." And with that, the goddess of love and beauty was gone again.

* * *

"Another brownie?" Grammy asked from across her little kitchen table for two.

"No thanks," Mylee said dully, as she absently ripped her napkin into tiny pieces.

"Babes, you had *nothing* to do with this trouble between your mom and dad."

"My head knows that, I guess, but...it just *feels* like if things were smoother between Mom and me, maybe she would have been happier and that would have made it easier for them to get along, know what I mean?"

Grammy shook her head in the negative. "If friction with a teen in the house caused marital stress, there would be no such thing as married parents of kids over the age of twelve. Butting heads with moms and dads is in the job description for teens. I'd actually be concerned if you didn't disagree with your mother from time to time."

Mylee continued her blank stare at her growing pile of napkin bits.

Grammy tried a different tactic. "What are you doing right now?"

Mylee's head shot up. "Sorry; I'll clean it up." She began to gather the evidence of her napkin massacre, prepared to throw it away.

"No. That's not what I mean, sweetheart. You stay right where you are. I mean, where are you?"

"Uh...here at your table?"

"Not sitting at home playing video games all day and night?"

"Noooo...."

"Not doing drugs? Not getting arrested?"

"No!"

"Not working your way to teen motherhood?"

"Grammy! *NO!*" Mylee was almost as mortified at the thought of discussing such a subject with her grandmother as she was at the prospect of doing it, to begin with.

"Uh-huh... How about your grades. D's and F's to start out your high-school career?"

"No, of course not! Last I checked, I still have A's in all my classes."

"So, let me see if I understand. You're an A-student who spends her time helping her grandmother with her laundry on a Thursday evening, you can't be described as a "screen-ager", you're not strung out on dope, you're not begging for bail money, you're not aspiring to have a starring role on *Teen Moms*, and your worst argument with your mother is that you want to participate in one sport and she wants you in another. And this sounds to you like someone who breaks up a marriage?"

Mylee couldn't help but laugh. "Well, when you put it like *that*..."

"Yeah. Pretty silly, huh?"

"Yeah, I guess." Mylee giggled again. Leave it to Grammy to sound totally '80s with "dope", totally 2010 with *Teen Moms*, and totally hip with "screen-ager". Man, she loved this woman!

"Feeling any more excited about the big game tomorrow?"

"Ugh. That whole thing has blown up into a total nightmare. The football game is just the tip of the iceberg. Sam sorta asked me to the Homecoming dance next weekend. Kinda...it was weird. Anyway, I didn't want to go with him. Not only do I have no real interest in the guy, but it has wrecked my friendship with Lilith. There's no knowing if we'll ever get *that* back. But Serena is all excited to 'live vicariously' through me because she's convinced Sam and I will end up being crowned Homecoming King and

Queen. Even Aphro—" Mylee caught herself before mentioning a certain Greek goddess she still wasn't convinced she had actually had conversations with. "I mean...lots of girls agree with Serena. Come to think of it, Lilith and Serena seem to represent the female Lakeview High School population pretty well. Half the girls stare daggers at me whenever I walk by in the halls, and the other half squeal and jump up and down, clapping their hands, telling me how lucky I am."

"But you don't want to be his date?"

"No, not really. Ty says I should do what I want, that if I don't feel like going out on a date I should follow my heart, 'because it's *your* life, dang it!' but that's okay. It's just one night. I think I can survive. Like Serena keeps telling me, it's kind of a fairytale-type story, right? So why not enjoy it?"

"Well...of the two I think I have to go with Tyler on this one."

"I'll have to tell him that." Mylee laughed. "You'd better be careful, though, or he might be asking *you* to the Homecoming dance. He was declaring his love for you again yesterday as he inhaled almost the entire batch of cookies I took to the gym." Grammy chuckled. Mylee continued, "But if you could have seen how much the news thrilled Mom, you'd understand why I haven't turned Sam down. It Lit. Her. UP!"

"Oh, Mylee, you can't let your mother's desires dictate who you date. You have to be your own person, doing what's right for *you*—just like you do with your trampoline and tumbling. If you want the truth of the matter, that's the root cause of your mom's current marital issues."

"Wait; I'm confused. I thought you just told me their 'break' doesn't have anything to do with me."

"It doesn't. It goes all the way back to when Sharron was in high school. She didn't learn to live for herself. She met your father, fell in love, and immediately started living for him—cheering him on at his games, hanging out with his friends, wearing what she thought he wanted her to wear, going to his college of choice,

throwing herself into projects like host-
ing his business Christmas party and
summer barbeque every year. That may
sound like it would work out if they're
both okay with it, but it's not healthy. It's
a poison that slowly splits a couple apart.
What your mother needs—not that she'd
ever listen to me—is to use this time to
discover *herself*. Either Paul will appreciate the woman she finds within, or he
won't. I hope he does, but if he doesn't,
she'll at least be able to go on, happy as
her own woman. You need to live for you,
Mylee. You can't have a successful relationship with someone else until you're
at peace with who you are."

"Oh...I didn't know..."

"Of course you didn't, sweetheart. We all
have challenges in our lives that we need
to work our way through. I have faith that
with this space and time to herself, Sharron will find her answers."

"I hope so. Thank you, Grammy; this has
helped a lot."

"Well, good! Now, let's make our way
back down to the laundry room. I bet

that load of whites in the dryer is done now."

* * *

Mylee's vision of the wet pavement blurred in the orange glow of the street lamps as she slowly walked through the chilly early-October rain on her way home from the bus stop. She pulled her hoodie further down over her forehead and wrapped her arms around her middle as her mind reeled with questions, insights, ideas, and more questions.

It was bizarre to think of her mom as a person, and not just "Mom"—a person who had tried so hard to make her relationship work, but in an entirely misguided way. It was sad to think that Mom hadn't felt confident enough over the years to be true to herself. What dreams and talents and passions had fallen to the wayside while Mom was so busy living for her husband and daughter? Could she help Mom find them again? In some ways, the way Grammy described her parents' marriage reminded Mylee of the way Aphrodite had described her relationship with Hephaestus. He seemed to devote his life to his wife, and instead of gratitude, her response was irritation and impatience with him. Is that how Dad was feeling about Mom? How could they fix that? She wasn't sure how, but she knew she had to try to help.

Mylee slipped her wet shoes off by the front door and made her way into the dark house, walking toward the blue glow of the television in the other room. Mom was, once again, on the sofa, blankly staring at the screen. Mylee doubted that if she shut the TV off and asked her mom what she had just been watching, Mom would have any idea. Her heart hurt at the realization that this uncharacteristic couch-potato behavior wasn't just her mom being depressed about trouble in her marriage. This was Mom not even knowing what to do with herself, now that she didn't have the marriage to focus on.

Mylee made her way to the kitchen and made some mac and cheese and a salad for both of them, ignoring Mom's insistence that she wasn't hungry. Satisfied when

Mom had eaten half of what Mylee had dished out for her, she cleaned up all the dishes, wished Mom a good night, and headed to her room.

"Well?" was the question Mylee received moments later, as soon as she raised the mirror to her face. "Did you come to your senses? How are things with you and Sexy Sam?"

"Hi, Aphrodite. I don't know. Fine, I guess," she offered with a non-committal shrug.

"Hmmm... You aren't sounding particularly enthusiastic. I thought you said he was *good looking* and *popular*."

"I did, and he is. It's just hard to get all excited about something that I'm really kinda doing for everyone else. Serena is all excited and seems to be having the time of her life, running around the school like a mad woman, trying to get everyone to get their votes in for Homecoming King and Queen. Mom is acting like it's her birthday, Mother's Day, and Valentine's Day all in one. She set up a

'Wardrobe War-Room' with Sam's mom, and they've already had an actual *meeting* to 'coordinate colors that will best accentuate' our 'seasons'—whatever *that* means."

"Youth today," Aphrodite muttered with a disappointed shake of her head. "Here you're being served not *only* a delicious little morsel of magnificent man, but you're getting some much-needed guidance on making the best of what you have so the poor boy won't run away screaming at the first glance of your appearance and apparel choice. No offense, of course," she added as an afterthought.

Mylee took a self-conscious look at her jeans and Spaceballs t-shirt. What was wrong with her clothes? She decided to change the subject. "Aphrodite, do you mind if I ask you a personal question?"

"Go ahead."

"Do you respect Hephaestus? When you talk about him, I get the sense that he annoys you, and I was just thinking about how sad that is for both of you."

Aphrodite appeared surprised by the query. "Respect him? I think he's incredibly talented. As you can see, he can make some jewelry and accessories that can *almost* come close to matching my beauty."

"Yeah," Mylee agreed. "This mirror is phenomenal. Was there a specific reason he made it for you?"

"He said that he wanted to craft a mirror that only showed true beauty. As I am the definition of true beauty, the mirror only shows me."

"Oh, so it's kinda like the magic mirror in *Snow White*?"

Aphrodite chuckled, then winked. "Where do you think The Brothers Grimm came up with that idea, darling?"

"Wow...fascinating! And so very romantic! ...But—sorry. I interrupted you before you could answer my question. Do you respect him?"

"I respect the work he does as an artist and metal worker. But...it's hard to keep my appreciation and respect for his talent in mind. First and foremost, I never *wanted* to be married to him. You can't force someone to love another; it just doesn't work that way. You end up resenting the person, and as unfair as that may be to the one you get forced to be with, it's no less true. On top of that, though, he spends all his time making me gifts. You'd think I would *adore* that, but...it got old. Really fast. I think if he did his own thing more often it would be easier for me to keep in mind the things I respect about him."

"Did he agree to help you make the fake caduceus?"

"Of course. He's working on it now."

"Maybe you can suggest he make something for *himself* next. You said he made your "Belt of Irresistibility". What if he made himself a magic accessory that helped you to better see and remember his attributes and accomplishments, as opposed to your resentment?"

Aphrodite regarded Mylee with another of her long, quiet stares. "You know, darling, you may be on to something there. I may do just that." She cocked her head to the side in contemplation. "Hmmm... I actually find myself enjoying our little chats. Who would have guessed?" Shaking off her deep thought, she advised, "Now get some sleep so you can wake early in the morning and try to do something with your hair...and find something acceptable to wear at that football game tomorrow night. Never forget—geek is *not* chic. Have fun, and I look forward to hearing all the juicy details!"

Chapter VII

Mylee

Text to Mylee from Serena: R u in?

Mylee: Yeah; just got thru the gate

Serena: Can't BELIEVE I had 2 babysit tonite!

Mylee: Me neither; REALLY could have used ur support here! & U call urself a friend! ☺

Serena: Hav u seen HIM yet?

Mylee: Nope. Lot more people here than I expected. Didn't know there were this many people into football.

Serena: Yeah; apparently it's a thing. What'd u end up wearing? Did u change after school?

Mylee: No. Still have Minecraft T on. Added Groot sweatshirt, tho

Mylee: & Gryffindor scarf cuz it's freakin' cold out here

Serena: Gryffindor! My, those r Bellevue's colors! Faux pas, gf, faux pas!

Mylee: What? How am I supposed to know who has what colors?!

Serena: Uh...ours r blu & white—that wudda been safe!

Mylee: Great. Now we're gonna lose cuz I'm a Hermione fan.

Serena: Just sayin'

Mylee: Just got ushered 2 my seat

Serena: OMG! What'd he say? What'd he do? Dish, woman, dish!

Mylee: He took pity on me & told me I could go home

Serena: WHAT?!

Mylee: Oh, sorry. That's just what I wished.

Mylee: He said "Prepare to be amazed. U r about 2 become my biggest fan." Poor guy's problem is he has no self-confidence.

Serena: LOL

Mom: Just chatted with Penny. She said she and Sam can give you a ride home after the game. Have fun! ☺

Mylee to Mom: But u said 2 just call when I'm ready 2 come home

Mom: Penny said she and Sam would be more than happy to take you home. I'm really tired, so I'd like to go to bed early. Behave yourself even though I won't be waiting up for you! ☺

Mylee to Mom: U could just come get me early so u can go 2 bed whenever u want

Mom: Nonsense; I wouldn't want to drag you away from your fun!

Mylee to Serena: Great. Just found out I'm gonna have 2 stay the whole game cuz Sam is my ride home.

Serena: The fairytale continues!

Mylee to Serena: A fairytale would have a curfew, like in Cinderella. This is gonna DRAGGGGGGG ONNNNNN

Ty: U @ the game?

Mylee to Ty: Yep. Nobody can say I haven't sacrificed 4 this school!

Ty: Feeling all jelly of the cheerleaders?

Mylee to Ty: Yeah. SO wish I could b wearing a skimpy mini skirt w/ them. Cuz it's so hot out. NOT! What r u up 2?

Ty: Watching paint dry.

Serena: I just had to change a blow-out diaper 😩🤮💩

Mylee to Serena: Jealous!

Serena: ???

Mylee to Serena: Sorry—wrong person.

Mylee to Ty: Jealous! Paint drying would b 10x more fun than this

Mylee to Ty: & much warmer, too. BONUS!

Ty: Dude, Bob Ross is THE MAN! Have u watched any of his shows on Netflix? His "happy little clouds" RULE!

Mylee to Ty: Oh; Caroline just showed me a Funco Pop figure she got last w/end that was a Deadpool Bob Ross. It was awesome! I need 2 check out his show

Serena: Ugh. Remind me to never have 1 of these little germ monsters of my own. Game start yet?

Mylee to Serena: Yeah, and WTH? Dad took me to a Sounders game last spring & it was a 90-minute game. I thought this was supposed to last an hour, but they keep STOPPING the flippin' clock?

Mylee to Serena: They should have told us 2 bring our sleeping bags, cuz @ this rate we won't even b leaving here tonite!

Serena: Sheesh! R they serving cheese w/ all ur WHINE?! Shall I give u a play-by-play of that last diaper change?

Serena: I can tell u w/ probably 100% accuracy everything the kid ate in the past 3 days. GROSS!!!

Mylee to Serena: LOL ok, ok, u win! Barely... ☺

Serena: The job should have come with a haddock suit

Mylee to Serena: A what?!

Serena: Ugh...stupid   autocorrect HAZ-MAT!

Mylee to Serena: I don't know. A haddock suit wudda been AWESOME! LOL!

Serena: BRB Gotta put munchkin to bed

Ty: Still @ the game?

Mylee to Ty: Stuck here til end of game. Have 2 get a ride home w/ Sam. Mom didn't want to wait up. ½ time now, tho, & I'm lovin' the marching band. They ROCK!

Ty: What?! Isn't there anyone else there who can take u home? U don't want 2 have 2 wait around 4 him after the game!

Mylee to Ty: I know, right?

Ty: Mum & Dad r out on a date, otherwise I know Mum would have picked u up. Want me 2 ask Ben 2 come get u?

Mylee to Ty: LOL like THAT would ever happen! Nah, I'm good. I'm tough. I got grit. ☺

Mylee to Ty: Ah, crud on a cracker. Forgot 2 charge my phone after school, & I'm down to 7%. C u @ the Homecoming decorating party tomorrow.

* * *

"Mylee! What a beautiful young lady you've grown up to be!"

Mylee looked to her left to find a woman who looked to be about Mom's age, totally decked out in blue and white, wearing a number-seven football jersey, and displaying LHS across her forehead in blue and white paint.

"Uh...thanks. Are you Sam's mom?"

"Sure am! You can call me Penny. Come on. Let's go over toward the locker room so we can wait for Sam to get changed," she exclaimed in a voice much too peppy and cheery after surviving the marathon football game that *Just. Wouldn't. Die!*

After they stood near the locker room doors for several awkward minutes, Sam made his way out. "Another phenomenal game, champ!" Sam's mom gushed, pulling him in for a side hug as they made their way to the car. "You lit up the whole field!"

Sam shot a cocky grin in Mylee's direction. She didn't want him getting the idea she was fangirling on him or anything—and run the risk of future game invitations—so she attempted to immediately dispel any potential misunderstandings. "Hope you don't mind having to swing me by my house on your way home; it appears your mom did my mom a solid and volunteered to take me home. Sorry. *Totally* not my choice."

Sam didn't seem to notice her intent at all. "Did you catch my play-action fake in the third? That sweet little spiral to Simpson for a quick six was a thing of beauty, wasn't it?"

Fudgsicle! Mylee didn't know she was going to get tested on the game! She scrambled to formulate a response that would not make it obvious that A) she had barely looked at the field at all aside from the halftime show, and B) had no idea what the heck he just said. Luckily, Sam's mom swooped in for the save. "Just one amazing play of many, Sam; you killed it out there! Bellevue didn't stand a chance!"

"Yeah!" Mylee added lamely, with a nod hopefully portraying confidence that she had any idea what she was talking about.

Sam called shotgun, so Mylee happily climbed into the back seat on her own. The drive consisted of more play-by-play breakdown of the game. Mother and son seemed content enough to banter back and forth, so Mylee just sat still and quiet, hoping nobody would make the effort to include her in the conversation.

"You gonna be there tomorrow to help with Homecoming decorations?" Sam asked as they approached Mylee's driveway. She nodded her head yes, then added a quiet "Yep" when she realized he probably couldn't see her in the dark.

"Oh, wonderful!" Sam's mom exclaimed happily. "That will give you two a chance to talk a little more! I thought about taking you kids out for ice cream or something tonight, but it's a little late. Maybe we can do something like that sometime soon, though."

"Oh, that's okay," Mylee assured. "I really appreciate the ride home, though; that was really nice of you."

"No problem at all, sweetheart. Have a good night, and Sam will see you tomorrow!"

"Okay. Thanks again. Good night!" Mylee called as she exited the car. She offered one last wave as she headed up the walk to her front door, and Sam's car pulled out of her driveway. Once in the house, she breathed a big sigh of relief, anxious to curl up under her blankets so she could warm up and get some much-needed sleep.

Chapter VIII

Ty

After some consistent badgering to hurry her up and get her out of the house, Ty finally got Mum to drop him off at the school twenty minutes early. The last he heard from Mylee had been the night before, when she was at the football game and her phone died. Did she get home okay? Did Sam hurt her in any way? Just as scary a thought, did she fall for Sam?

Ty found the gym door locked, so he stood under the overhang to get out of the rain while he waited for the custodian to open the school. He felt like he was coming out of his skin with anxiety; he still had no answers. When he called her a few times that morning, they all went straight to voicemail. Did she just forget to charge her phone? Was it smashed on the side of the road in the massive accident she got in on her way home? Was she having some sort of breakdown because of everything going on with her mom and dad? When Mylee told him about her dad moving out, Ty felt horrible for her—especially since it happened at the same time her grandmother moved across town. He didn't even know what to say; he couldn't imagine how devastating it would be if his parents split up. Add the loss of one of her best friends, and no wonder she was walking around looking like a zombie, stressed out and getting no sleep. Had she run away from home because she just couldn't take it anymore? Had she been kidnapped? He shook his head, trying to pull the brake on his runaway train of panicked thoughts.

He kicked himself for not considering that he wouldn't be able to actually get into the school early—especially since it was now pouring cats and dogs out. It wasn't the usual Pacific Northwest misty shower. It was a downpour, like in Florida when they visited Disney World for his tenth birthday.

Finally, he was allowed inside, and other students started drifting in. Serena was one of the first to show up. She hadn't heard from Mylee since last night, either, but Ty found himself irritated with her lukewarm level of concern over the matter. Sam showed up a few minutes later, but Ty didn't want to invite an argument by asking him about Mylee's whereabouts. At least Sam's presence proved they hadn't crashed on the way home from the football game. And Mylee hadn't shown up with Sam, hanging off his arm, looking all googly-eyed in love, so there was that to be thankful for.

When she was fifteen minutes late, Ty knew there was a problem. She was early or on time for everything. Mylee wouldn't be late, and in the very unlikely event she was, she would have let someone know she was running late. No. Something was wrong. What to do? He didn't have her mother's number to call and ask her what was going on. "Serena, do you have Mylee's mom's number?"

"No, why?"

"I'm worried that she isn't here yet and hasn't let either of us know why or where she is."

"You're right; this isn't exactly like her. Hey, Sam!" Serena yelled across the gym. "Did Mylee say anything last night about not coming today?"

"Nope. She said she'd be here," he said, shaking his head as he walked over to her.

"Something must be wrong," Ty said in a voice tight with worry. "She wouldn't just flake on us."

"Ah, relax," Sam chided him. "She's a big girl. I'm sure she's fine. She'll get here when she's good and ready." With that he moved on to another group of students, apparently bored with the conversation.

Ty looked over at Serena. Chewing worriedly on her thumb nail, she admitted, "I think you're right, Ty. We should have seen or heard from her by now. What should we do?"

"Don't worry about it," Ty said. "Go get started with everyone on the decorations, and I'll take care of this...one way or another." With that, he pulled his phone out of his pocket and made his way to the hallway. Mylee had said she was going to

Big Finn Hill Park for a fundraiser before coming to school, but she said the event would end well before she was supposed to be here. Mum and Dad were helping Uncle Jimmy move, so they weren't around to give him a ride. That left one last option. He sighed in preparation for a fight.

"What?" Ben demanded when he answered the phone. This wasn't a good start.

"Would you mind giving me a ride? I need to run up to Big Finn Hill Park to look for Mylee."

"Pff...not happenin'. I go into work at four, and I don't plan to move from this couch until I have to."

"Come on, dude! What if I pay you for gas—and your time. I have twenty dollars on me. What if I give that to you?"

"Nope."

Ty blew out a frustrated sigh. Running a hand through his hair, he tried to think of anything else he had to bargain with.

"What about your chores? What if I do your chores for you for a week?"

"Still not worth it."

"A month, then. Twenty dollars plus your chores for a month."

"You're telling me you're going to pay me twenty bucks *plus* do all the poop-scooping, recycling, and vacuuming for a *month*?"

"That's exactly what I'm telling you."

"You got yourself a deal, lil' bro! You're at the school?"

"Yeah. Hurry! Please."

* * *

Mylee

"Are you sure we can't give you a lift home?" D.J.'s dad offered again as he loaded the back of his car with the table they used for the dried flower sale.

"Thanks so much, but no. My dad should be here any minute to pick me up," Mylee assured him.

"Okay. If you're sure."

"Yup." She smiled.

"Thanks again for joining us," said D.J. "We made a lot more than I expected!"

"It was my superb flower-arranging skills," piped up D.J.'s friend and fellow gardening club member, May.

"He would kill me if he ever heard me say it, but I think Hudson's were the prettiest arrangements." D.J. giggled.

"He did have quite an eye for color coordination," Mylee agreed.

With everything loaded into the car, D.J.'s dad said, "Okay, girls, time to head out. I told May's mom I'd have her home in time for her violin lesson, so we need to get moving."

"Nice meeting you," said May as she climbed into D.J.'s car.

"If you ever want to do some gardening with us, just text me and I can give you the day, time, and address," D.J. reminded Mylee as she climbed into the car after May.

"Will do!" Mylee smiled again, waving goodbye.

Then she was alone at the park, watching her new friends drive away. She sat down on the grass, confident Dad would be there in no time. D.J. had mentioned texting. Mylee couldn't believe she forgot to charge her phone. She felt incomplete without it. It would have been so much more assuring to have shot off a text to Dad, letting him know the sale was over and she was ready any time he was. She wondered how kids from earlier generations lived with so much uncertainty in their lives!

She looked down at her arm to see two distinct splatters from rain drops. She looked up at the sky. *Come on, Dad; hurry up*, she silently begged. She didn't see his car coming around the bend in the road, though, and raindrops were beginning to attack at a faster pace, so she ran to the little equipment shed next to the ballfield. The door was locked, but there was an overhang that she figured would protect her from the rain just fine until Dad showed up. She thought about laying into him for being so late. She'd really give him a piece of her mi—

She screamed. She batted and shook and clawed at her clothes. She had stepped right into a massive spider web, and she just *knew* she had a dozen or more killer arachnids crawling all over her. She flipped her hands frantically through her hair, desperately trying to rid herself of the hundreds of creepy, crawly legs she felt prowling with deadly purpose all over her scalp. She sprinted away from the shed, out to the middle of the open field, petrified of getting caught in another of the many webs she was positive riddled the shed.

Rain was now pouring down, one of the hardest rains she had ever seen. Figures; it was just her luck. She hoped it was just a quick cloud burst, because her sweatshirt wouldn't be able to hold up long under such an assault. Still hyperventilating, she tried to focus on calming her breathing. She had no watch on to tell her just how late Dad was, but her wait was beginning to feel way too long, and she was nervous about what she would do if he didn't show. She was too far from home to walk. She knew Grammy Jean's new home was somewhere nearby, but she wasn't sure about the directions. She didn't know where the closest bus stop was, but that didn't matter, anyway; she didn't have her bus pass or any money. Why, oh *why* hadn't she taken D.J.'s dad up on his offer for a ride home?

* * *

Ty

"Okay, so *where* are we going?" Ben asked impatiently as Ty quickly climbed into the passenger seat, shaking water out of his hair after his dash from the school building to the car.

"Big Finn Hill Park."

"And why are we going to the park in the middle of this hurricane?"

"Because that's the last place I know Mylee was supposed to be before she was supposed to meet us at the school."

"Dude, you've got it so bad for this chick," Ben said with a snort and a shake of his head. "You know you don't have a chance with her, right? You'll never be anything more than just a permanent resident of her Friend Zone."

"Shut up!" Ty was too worried to think about the title of his relationship with Mylee. He didn't care what he was to her at this point; as long as she was safe, that's all that mattered.

Ben had his windshield wipers on full blast, and Ty still had a hard time seeing anything. As they pulled into the parking lot, he desperately scanned for any sign of Mylee. Looking out toward what looked to be a baseball field, he frantically wiped the condensation away from his window. Then he saw it. There was a dark shape in the middle of the field. He didn't know if it was her, but he had to check it out.

"Hold on a minute. I'll be right back," he practically shouted as he jumped out of the car. "Mylee!" he yelled as he ran into the field.

He could see it now. It *was* a person he had spotted. A person huddled in the middle of the flooding field with arms wrapped around knees, now jumping up off the ground and—YES! It was Mylee. *"Ty!"* she screeched as she barreled toward him. Meeting somewhere in the middle, they threw themselves into a huge hug.

Mylee burst into tears, nearly choking him with her arms wrapped around his neck. "Ohmygod, Ty," she sobbed. "Thank you so much for coming. I thought everyone had forgotten all about me!"

Ty pulled himself away and held her at arm's length. "Are you okay?" he demanded.

"Yeah. Just soaked...and freezing," she admitted with chattering teeth.

"Come on; let's get you to the car."

They ran to the car and hopped into the back seat. "Hi, Ben," Mylee managed around another sob.

"Mylee! Are you okay?" Ben asked, showing more concern than Ty had ever seen from his brother.

Mylee nodded her head as she struggled to click her seatbelt with shaking hands.

"Wait a sec. Before you buckle in—*here*."
Ty pulled off his sweatshirt. "Take yours
off and put this one on. It's a little damp,
but it'll keep you a heck of a lot warmer
than your drenched one will."

"Here," Ben chimed in as he handed back
his flannel shirt. "I just turned the heat
up to high, but I don't know how much
you'll feel it back there."

Mylee struggled out of her wet sweatshirt, put Ty's on, and spread Ben's shirt
over her legs like a blanket. By the time
she was done changing, her crying had
subsided to just an occasional sniffle. She
got her seatbelt fastened, and Ben slowly
pulled out of the parking lot.

"Where are we headed?" he asked.

"Um...I'm not sure," Mylee said, still snif-
fling. "I don't know where anybody is. I
don't know what Mom had planned for
this afternoon. Dad was supposed to pick
me up; then I was going to hang with
him for a while, and he was going to drop
me off at the school, but..." Mylee's tears
started back up. "He never showed," she

whispered, covering her face with her hands and shaking her head.

"That's okay. We'll go back to our place and sort it all out. Just try to relax; we've gotcha," Ben assured in a calming voice. Ty was amazed by his brother's transformation.

Ty grabbed Mylee's freezing red hands and held them between his as they made their way to his house. "Why were you in the middle of the field?" he asked gently. "There were trees you could have stood under to help protect you from the rain, and I think I saw a little shed, too."

"I tried the shed," explained Mylee, "but I was ruthlessly attacked by a whole horde of spiders in a massive network of webs. I panicked and just stayed out in the open, where I knew there likely wouldn't be any more around to assault me."

Ty concentrated on not letting his smile show. How anyone could be so freaked out by a little bug, he had no idea, but he knew Mylee would be all triggered if he laughed at her or told her she was crazy. Instead, he rubbed her hands reassuringly and turned his attention out the window. He was surprised to see his Dad's car as they pulled into the driveway. "I thought he they were helping Uncle Jimmy today." He turned questioning eyes to Ben.

"I thought so, too. They weren't here when I left."

As they made their way through the door, Mum ran over, exclaiming, "Oh, Mylee! Sweetheart! What happened?"

"She got stuck out at Big Finn Hill Park for a little bit," Ty answered for Mylee, as he didn't think she'd be able to get words through her chattering teeth.

"Poor dear! Well, let's get you warmed up. Ty, go grab a pair of sweatpants, a t-shirt, and a warm sweatshirt from your room. Mylee, you come with me. We have a heat lamp in the master bathroom that we'll turn on while you get changed. I have a nice, thick pair of socks you can put on, too. Ben, please go get an extra blanket and the heating pad from the hall closet and get it plugged in by the couch and turned on to the warmest setting."

Everyone broke to do as Mum instructed. Ty hoped Mylee would be back to her smiling self soon; he couldn't bear to see her cold, scared, and sad much longer. He frantically searched through clothes, looking for the warmest and cleanest he could find. Why, oh why hadn't he done the load of laundry Mum had been nagging him to do last weekend? Finding acceptable articles that fit the description of Mum's demands, he ran for his parents' room for Mum to hand everything off to Mylee. He made one quick stop at his bathroom along the way, though. "I got you some dry clothes," he yelled through the master bath door, "and I brought you my brush, too, in case you had any—" He caught himself before he said "webs," knowing that might freak her out all over again, "—Any lingering *stuff* you might want to brush out of your hair."

"Thanks, Ty," was the quiet, muffled response he got through the bathroom door.

A few minutes later they were all back in the living room, Mylee lying on the couch

with three blankets and one Pugly covering her, Ty sitting at the end of the couch
with Mylee's feet on his lap, and Mum in
the chair next to them. Ben apparently
decided the situation was under control,
so he made his way back down to his
"apartment" in the basement to get ready
for work.

"I didn't think you'd be home," Ty said,
directing the comment to Mum.

"We didn't plan to be. We helped Uncle
Jimmy with the first load to his new place,
but then the deluge started and there was
no way we could reload the truck, so we
decided to wait until the storm passes."

Mum turned her attention to his friend.
"So, Mylee, what were you doing at the
park, sweetheart?" Her voice was quiet
and soothing.

"I was helping at a fundraiser. Luckily
it ended before the rain began, but I
don't understand; Dad was supposed to
pick me up when it ended, but he never
showed. I didn't have my phone with me,
and I didn't know what to do, so I waited,

hoping he was just running late...like... really, *really* late."

"Here, My." Ty handed her his phone. "Why don't you call him or your mom to find out what happened. I'll be right back; I'm gonna go make us some hot chocolate."

When he returned with two steaming mugs of chocolatey, marshmallowey delicious-ness, Mylee explained that it had been a case of her mom thinking her dad was going to pick her up and her dad thinking her mom was going to do it. She said they both felt horrible about the mix-up. Her mom would be over shortly to pick her up, and her dad planned to spend the entire next day with Mylee, doing whatever she wanted, to make it up to her.

Next, they called Serena and put her on speakerphone, so they could let her know Mylee was okay. Before long, Ty and Ser-ena had Mylee laughing so hard she was snorting—even worse than Pugly usually did—then laughing harder over being caught snorting. Ty breathed a huge sigh of relief. All was right with the world again.

Chapter IX

Mylee

"I don't know what we're going to do," Mom fretted as she sat down at the table with her plate of lasagna.

"What do you mean?" Mylee asked as she cut hers up into bites to help it cool faster.

"Well, I planned on going out with you tomorrow to get your dress for Homecoming next weekend. Penny even planned to tag along, to help with color and style selection so you and Sam will complement each other best. But now you're going to be spending the day with Dad, and I just don't know if we'll have time to shop properly."

"Don't worry about it, Mom. I plan on wearing the dress I got for Meghann's wedding."

Mom made a disgusted sound in the back of her throat. "You can't wear the same dress you wore to your cousin's wedding!"

"Why not? I like it and it fits fine. And nobody at school has even seen me in it!"

"But what if it doesn't coordinate well with Sam's suit?"

"Yeah. About that." Mylee paused for a fortifying breath. "Mom, I know you were really excited about the idea of Sam and me going to Homecoming together, but I've decided not to go with him." She winced, bracing herself for her mother's response.

"I don't understand. What do you mean? Why would you not want to go to Homecoming? —and not with just *anyone*, but a handsome guy who will almost certainly be crowned Homecoming King? Did he hurt you somehow? Do something rude?"

"No, nothing like that. I never planned on going to the dance with anyone except my friends. Sam's nice enough, but I'm just not really...interested in him right now. I decided to go with him anyway because I knew it would make you happy, but Aph—uh...a friend of mine was with a guy to make someone else happy, and all she ended up doing was resenting the guy she had to be with. I don't really know Sam all that well, but it wouldn't be fair if I ended up resenting him because I felt pressured into going on a date. I'm really, really sorry, because I know you were looking forward to it, but..." She pulled her freshly charged phone out of her back pocket. "I think I've found something you can look forward to, instead, that would make you even happier."

Chancing a glance up at her mom, she found a confused stare with just a hint of hurt, so she forged on. "I found this ad online yesterday, Mom." She handed the phone over to her mother. "The Kirkland Girls and Boys Club is looking for a volunteer cheerleading coach for middle-school-aged girls. I called the number they listed, and apparently the woman who held the position had to suddenly move out of state for her husband's work. They're really desperate. They have a team of super-excited girls, but they've been without a coach for a whole week now, and they'll have to shut the program down if they don't find a replacement right away. When I talked about your experience and love for the sport, the woman I was talking to practically did a cheer over the phone, she was so happy. They thought you'd be a perfect fit! I told them I'd talk to you, and if you agreed to fill the position, that you would call them back Monday."

Mom looked somewhat shell-shocked. Between the residual guilt and stress over the park incident from earlier in the day, the unexpected blow from her announcement about her Homecoming decision and the out-of-nowhere job proposal, Mylee figured Mom didn't even know where to begin with any type of response. She thought she'd try to make it easier for her. She didn't want Mom feeling bad, so she focused only on the positive. "You have tonight and all day tomorrow to think about coaching. I really think you should do it, though, Mom. You *rock* at cheering and it's something you're passionate about. This would give you a chance to share that passion with girls who may lose *their* opportunity to make happy memories like you did on your teams."

Mom's expression suddenly transformed into the excited, plotting face Mylee associated with clothes shopping and photo shoots. With any hope, that meant her preoccupation with Homecoming—and maybe even her struggling marriage—might soon be behind her, replaced with feeling needed and appreciated.

"Well...it would be such a shame if those poor girls had to give up their dream of cheering," Mom quietly mused.

Mylee decided she'd just let that seed grow. She finished her last few bites of dinner, took care of her dishes, and excused herself. Mom looked even happier than before. Mylee smiled as she made her way to her bedroom.

* * *

"Hello?"

"Welcome back to the world of living with a phone," greeted Serena.

"OMG, I *totally* learned my lesson. I'll never forget to charge it again," promised Mylee.

"You didn't forget because you were all distracted by thoughts of you and Sam, were you?"

"No. I had to check in with Aph—uh...Dad. I had to check in with Dad to, uh, make sure he was all set to pick me up this afternoon."

"Hmmm...strange that he couldn't remember from last night to today that he was the one who was supposed to get you," observed Serena.

"Yeah, strange," Mylee agreed, thinking with a bitter shake of her head just how much better her day would have gone if she *had* called her dad to confirm that he would pick her up from the park. Another lesson learned, she guessed.

"Well...how *are* you feeling about Sam?" Serena quizzed.

"I don't know. He's totally into himself, but he's nice enough, I guess. Why? What's with these questions?"

"Ummm...I'm starting to wonder if I ever should have been encouraging you to go to Homecoming with him," Serena admitted.

"What? Why?"

"Well...he was really acting like a player today at the decorating party. I knew you weren't necessarily thinking of dating him after the dance, but it just seemed really *rude* that he'd be hitting on other girls when you weren't there. Especially when we were all worried that something had happened to you. He hadn't declared his love for you or anything, but if he was truly interested in you, it seems he would have at least *asked* about you, instead of...well...what he *did* do."

"What did he do?"

"To start with, he flirted shamelessly with Lilith."

"Oh. Well...that's not a bad thing. We both know that—unlike me—she *is* really interested in Sam," Mylee reasoned.

"Yeah, but there were all sorts of whispers about how he couldn't be very happy with you if he was going after someone else less than a day after your first date."

"First of all, last night wasn't a date. Second, I don't care what people have to say about it. Let them think whatever they want. If Lilith will be happy with him, I'm all for them getting together."

"Oh, she wants nothing to do with him."

"Wait, what? I thought she liked him!"

"She did...until she saw how he treated you."

"He didn't treat me any way! He invited me to a football game, I watched it, and he and his mom took me home. Where's the 'treating'?"

"She said she wanted to talk to you about that herself. She wanted me to talk to you first, though, because she worried you would hang up on her. Is it okay if she gives you a call?"

"Of course," Mylee said, still utterly confused.

A few minutes later Mylee's phone rang again and the screen, indeed, read "Lilith".

"Hello?"

"Hi," Lilith greeted with a distinctly sad note to her voice. "Thanks for letting me call you. And Mylee, I'm so, so sorry!" She began to cry.

"Hey," Mylee gently soothed, "no crying. It's okay. What's going on?"

After getting her tears somewhat under control, Lilith explained. "Sam asked you to Homecoming and I was mad, thinking you must have been encouraging him to like you, somehow." She paused to blow her nose. "I mean, why would he ask you to Homecoming if he didn't really like you, right? Then he was flirting with me all over the place today, and I was furious! How dare he ask you to the dance, then start hitting on me?! Any guy who disrespects a girl like that...well, I certainly don't want anything to do with him! I told him to buzz off."

"Good for you," Mylee encouraged.

"Yeah, but you know what? He buzzed right over...to *Olivia*. I think they may have even kissed in the hall. Can you believe that!?"

"Olivia from the cheerleading team?"

"Yeah."

"Huh." Mylee considered all Lilith had told her. "She was giving me some serious stink eye last night at the game. Guess this helps to explain that."

"I'm not trying to tell you what to do about Homecoming. You have every right to go with him if you want. I suppose you should be prepared, though, just in case he un-invites you to the dance so he can take Olivia instead. I just wanted to apologize for yelling at you the other day. I was way out of line, and I wouldn't blame you if you hate me now, but I just thought at least I owed you the truth about today."

"I forgive you. As for the dance, I've already decided to tell Sam I won't be going with him. Thank you for telling me about what happened today, though. You know, Grammy Jean told me that sometimes crushes can squash out the ability to think straight. Maybe that's why they're called 'crushes'." Both girls giggled. "She told me to be patient, though, because you would surely come back to your senses and your friendship is too valuable to give up on."

"I'm glad you listened to her. Your Grammy Jean is a brilliant woman."

"Yes, she is," Mylee agreed. "She most definitely is."

The girls chatted for a few more minutes, catching up on all they hadn't talked about in the few days they were apart. Mylee ended the call feeling like a weight had been lifted from her chest. She was so glad their little group was back to being best buds, like they should be, and she genuinely looked forward to Homecoming with them, knowing they'd have a great time with lots of laughs.

She picked the mirror up with a smile.

"Well, look at you!" greeted Aphrodite. "With your big smile and even bigger glow to your cheeks! I'm guessing you had a Sam-tacular time today, darling?"

Mylee burst out laughing, and it took her a little time to pull herself together. "Well, it has certainly been a memorable day, but it didn't have anything to do with Sam."

Aphrodite looked confused. "I can't think of anything that could match the pure joy of time spent with a handsome young man—such as your Sam. What else could it possibly be? You did see him today at the school, didn't you?"

"No. I never made it to the school—long story, don't ask—so I didn't end up seeing Sam. I'm happy for a few great reasons. One, I think I may have found a way to help my mom. And two, I got my friend Lilith back today. I had been missing her terribly."

Aphrodite's expression was a mix of disgust and horror. "Wasn't that the girl who said all sorts of nasty things about you because of Sam's interest in you? Why ever would you consider being friends with her again?"

"Lilith was angry the other day, and she was just speaking out of that anger. She apologized today, and I forgave her because she's been a good friend since the second grade and everyone makes mistakes."

"So, she is fine with you going to the dance with Sam now?" Aphrodite asked with a skeptical raise of her eyebrow.

"She told me she would have been. But I decided to turn Sam down."

"Maybe that flush to your cheeks is due to fever. You must be ill; I can't think of any rational reason not to *jump* at the chance to enter the dance on that young man's arm!"

"It was actually you who convinced me to tell him no."

"*What*?!" Aphrodite exclaimed. "Now I *know* you've come down with something, because I *never* said any such thing!"

"No, I know you encouraged me to go to Homecoming with Sam. I decided to not go with him after hearing your story about how much you grew to resent Hephaestus. It was never anything Hephaestus did to you. I didn't want to do that to Sam. I know you and Mom thought it would be good for me to go with him, but *I* didn't think so. If I went as Sam's date, I might have held that against him. Plus,

I just learned he's a total player, and I don't want anything to do with that."

Again Aphrodite stared silently at Mylee. She tilted her head to one side, appeared to consider what Mylee said, then tilted it to the other side and seemed to contemplate further. These long silences were becoming regular enough that Mylee wasn't even uncomfortable with them anymore. "You know, darling, you and I see the world through very different eyes. I am intrigued by your views. While I am anxious to have my mirror returned to me, I would enjoy having more chats with you. As it turns out, that will be possible with a gift left for you in the mirror's place."

"You're giving me a gift?"

"Not me, darling. Hephaestus. He so appreciated your suggestion to make himself an accessory—he chose a magnificent ring—that he also made you a golden necklace featuring a beautiful ruby rose. The best part is that if you look in a mirror while wearing it and call my name, we'll be able to continue our chats."

"Wow! I don't even know what to say! Please tell him thanks for me and give him an extra hug!"

"Ha! Hugging Hephaestus is something I never would have considered. Now I can honestly say I will pass on your thanks, as well as your hug," Aphrodite said with a smile. "Good night for now, darling, and should you wish, we can talk again, sometime soon."

Chapter X

Ty

Ty rounded the corner to the freshman hallway and stopped short, his eyebrows shooting up in surprise at the sight before him: further down the hall, his crew. His peeps. All of them...including Lilith. And all three girls were laughing and smiling. It was awesome seeing the whole gang back together, but he wondered what happened to fix everything blown apart between Mylee and Lilith.

He feared, however, that whatever truce had been worked out would now fall back apart. Sam was heading toward them from the other direction.

"Hey, Mylee," Sam the Snake spoke, turning the girls' heads his direction as Ty joined the group. "Can I talk to you for a minute?"

"Oh, hi, Sam. Yeah, I was going to look for you at lunch. I need to talk to you, too. Um, maybe we should step into Ms. Duarte's room, so we can talk alone?"

Sam and Mylee walked across the hall and entered the empty classroom. Ty shot a questioning glance toward Serena and Lilith.

"No need to worry about anything, Ty," Serena consoled. "This is just Mylee kickin' Sam to the curb." Lilith nodded in confirmation with a smile.

Ty had to concentrate on not yelling, "*YES!*" at the top of his lungs, running down the hall, jumping in the air, doing fist pumps and a complex, over-the-top, obnoxious touchdown dance.

"Hey!" Serena interrupted his fantasy. "There aren't many people out here yet, and it sounds like they're just inside the door. If we stand right over there just outside the door, we may be able to hear what's going on—you know...to make sure Mylee is safe and all."

With two quick nods of agreement, all three tip-toed to the partly closed classroom door to eavesdrop.

"What?!" Sam could be heard exclaiming.

"Yeah. Sorry. I realize it's less than a week before the dance, and I wouldn't be saying this if I had any doubt you'd be able to find another date in time, but I'm positive that won't be an issue, so it's all good, right? Oh, and I made sure I was taken off the list of candidates for Homecoming Queen, so there won't be any awkward moments in the unlikely event I won."

"But *why* would you not want to go with me?"

"It's not you. It's just...the circumstances weren't right. I'm sure you'll end up having a much better time with someone else."

"Pff...well, I *know* it's not me. I'm just struggling to think of anything that *would* lead to you breaking it off."

"Well...technically I'm not breaking anything off. You never *asked* me to Homecoming, and I never said yes. I told you I'd *think* about it. I've thought about it and this is just me answering you...*with a no.*"

Mylee sounded like she was clamping down on some growing annoyance. "What was it you wanted to talk to me about, anyway?" she asked, as if trying to steer the conversation in a less irritating direction or even wrap up the whole chat altogether.

Sam chuckled, then paused. Mylee's friends leaned in to catch what he had to say. "I was coming to tell you I've decided to take Olivia to Homecoming. I suppose I have you to thank. She wasn't giving me the time of day, but then she got good and jealous when I invited you to the game the other night, so she finally came around."

Ty held his breath, feeling horrible for his closest friend, who just learned she had been used. He clenched his fists and gritted his teeth, desperately wanting to go in and show Sam just how un-cool that was. Mylee finally spoke up. "Huh...Suddenly you're reminding me of something Serena described the other night." Ty was relieved to not hear any sign of quiver, tears, or pain in her voice.

"Oh yeah? What's that?"

"A big bag of Pampers—self-absorbed and full of crap."

Aw SNAP! thought Ty with glee. Lilith turned to look at him and mouthed "*Daaaaannnnggg*" with raised eyebrows. Serena silently snapped her fingers in front of her face in the universal "oh no she *di'int*" movement. Then all three realized Mylee's burn likely meant they'd be caught listening if they didn't get their butts away from the door. They leaped and scuffled across the hall, spun, and leaned as casually as they could against the lockers.

Mylee emerged first, shaking her head and rolling her eyes, and made her way across the hall to her friends. Sam followed her out, paused for a moment to sneer at Ty, then turned and walked in the direction he had come. Serena and Lilith group-hugged Mylee, jumping up and down, peppering her with a flurry of squealing, laughing, and encouragement.

"You were *ah-MAZ-ing* in there!"

"You *ROCK*, girlfriend!"

"That. Was. *BRILLIANT!*"

Ty couldn't think of a better way to start off his week.

* * *

"Hi Ben." Mylee greeted his brother with a big, beautiful smile. Ty shook his head as he climbed in the back seat next to her. Would the poor girl never learn?

"Hey, Mylee; feeling better?" Ben asked as he turned his head to face her...*with a smile*. No *way!* Ty couldn't believe it. He should have suspected that Ben had been replaced by some shape-shifting alien lifeform that morning when he pardoned Ty from paying him back for the ride. Ty had decided to abort his cream cheese in the deodorant stick idea, but oh, it was *so* back on now!

Maybe if he just clicked his seatbelt on like nothing had happened, Mylee wouldn't notice Ben's response. Nope. His luck for the day had run out. She laughed delightedly and, spinning so she could face Ty full-on, she answered, "Oh yeah, Ben. Thanks for asking! Today has been *great,* and it's getting nothing but better!" She leaned closer and whispered, "I'm a fan of snickerdoodles, by the way. With just a slight sprinkle of cinnamon on top."

Then she proceeded to do a celebratory seat dance for the next three miles, complete with a side to side body wave, the sprinkler, a little Gangnam style, an Egyptian head roll, some shoulder flick action...she even dabbed. Ty acted totally irritated about losing the bet and having to put up with her gloating, but on the inside, he was eating it up. She was absolutely adorable as she danced. If he got this treatment with every bet he lost, he'd be sure to make bets with her often and plan to lose every time!

* * *

Mylee

Mylee spent a spectacular Sunday with Dad. They checked out MoPOP— Museum of Pop Culture—walked around Seattle Center for a while, and enjoyed an awesome dinner out together. It was nice to share so many laughs and be reminded that nothing had changed between them. They planned on going to the movies next Sunday.

With the gang back together, Mylee looked past the fiasco with Sam and vowed to stay true to herself and her friends. Lilith didn't seem awkward about what happened with Sam in the least. They even planned a sleepover with Serena Friday night at Lilith's house, so they could all get ready for Saturday's dance together.

Tramp and tumble practice went great. She landed a tumbling triple back handspring, back layout that, with a little more practice, might rival Ty's in power and height. She couldn't wait for the competition season to start back up. She hoped they'd do well enough to make it to Regionals again. Heck, they could make it all the way to Nationals!

She noticed Ty was looking at her a bit differently during practice. Maybe he was seeing her in new ways. Maybe he was remembering how much they had meant to each other over the years. Whatever it was, Mylee was just thankful to have him in her life.

She had won her bet with him—she giggled as she thought back on his response to her celebration dance in the car. She loved that Ty could always make her laugh, always knew when she *needed* to laugh, but also always knew how to be there for her in other ways, too—like when he rescued her from the park. If she had felt like going on a date to Homecoming, *that's* the guy she would have chosen. Maybe some future dance...

After practice, she got a text from Mom, who was super-psyched, celebrating landing the job as the new coach. She was using all caps, lots of exclamation points, and whole strings of smiles, party hats, and firework emojis. Go, Mom!

When she got home, she found in place of Aphrodite's mirror the most beautiful necklace ever. Hephaestus had outdone himself with a stunning ruby-red rose and a golden stem that she would cherish the rest of her life. She thought about trying to use it to reach Aphrodite as the goddess mentioned, maybe with the pewter hand mirror she grabbed from Grammy Jean's box, but she decided to wait until she could give her an update on the Homecoming dance. She didn't want to bother the goddess too often.

Instead, she carefully clasped the gorgeous gold chain of the necklace around her neck, shut off her light, and snuggled into bed. She smiled, breathed deep, and hummed out a happy, relaxed, and satisfied breath.

She felt more at peace than she had in days, and she truly looked forward to her days yet to come.

About the Author

Ellie Collins

Ellie Collins wrote her multi-award-winning debut novel, **Daisy, Bold & Beautiful**, when she was turning eleven and just beginning sixth grade. She finished writing **Mylee**, the second in her Greek mythology fantasy series, before heading back to school for seventh grade and turning twelve. She writes amid a very busy extra-curricular schedule, including a spot on both a gymnastics team and a trampoline and tumbling team, as well as taking weekly piano lessons. She's an avid gamer who loves hanging out with friends. Her love of Greek mythology inspires her writing.

www.facebook.com/AuthorEllieCollins/

Fresh Ink Group

Publishing
Free Memberships
Share & Read Free Stories, Essays, Articles
Free-Story Newsletter
Writing Contests

✺

Books
E-books
Amazon Bookstore

✺

Authors
Editors
Artists
Professionals
Publishing Services
Publisher Resources

✺

Members' Websites
Members' Blogs
Social Media

Twitter: @FreshInkGroup
Google+: Fresh Ink Group
Facebook.com/FreshInkGroup
LinkedIn: Fresh Ink Group
About.me/FreshInkGroup
FreshInkGroup.com

Fresh Ink Group

Also by Ellie Collins!

D.J. and her dad moved far from the small town and only home she ever knew. Now she's starting middle school in the city with kids she's never met. She tries to make friends, but they all appear to be slaves to screen time. D.J. just likes to garden, nurturing plants, watching them grow and thrive. It seems she'll never find a way to fit in, but then she awakens in a gorgeous garden where she meets Persephone, Goddess of Spring. She must be dreaming; her new friend can't possibly be real—and what could she know about getting along with gamers? D.J. really needs some ideas, or she might never find her own place in a complicated world.

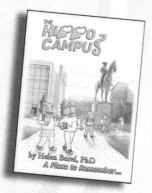